escape FROM FilM SchOOl

A NOVeL

Harlan
write on

escape from film school

A novel

RICHARD WALTER

Thomas Dunne books
St. Martin's Griffin
New York

This novel is fully and wholly a work of fiction in every aspect and detail. While actual names of some public figures are used, all incidents, anecdotes, events, situations, characters, and dialogue are strictly the author's invention.

THOMAS DUNNE BOOKS.
An imprint of St. Martin's Press.

Design by Maureen Troy

www.stmartins.com

Library of Congress Cataloging-in-Publication Data

Walter, Richard.
    Escape from film school : a novel / Richard Walter.
        p.   cm.
    ISBN 0-312-20537-6 (hc)
    ISBN 0-312-26731-2 (pbk)
    I. Title.
PS3573.A4722836E83   1999
813'.54—dc21   99-21993
                                                                                    CIP

10 9 8 7 6 5 4 3 2

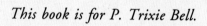

This book is for P. Trixie Bell.

ACKNOWLEDGMENTS

SPECIAL THANKS TO MY editor, Melissa Jacobs, for her faith, wisdom, consideration, and courage; to my agent, Jane Dystel, every author's dream, a warrior for writers and writing; and to Miriam Goderich for her creative insight and support.

A warm *mahalo* to John and Shannon Tullius for creating the Maui Writers Conference, for hosting me and the clan year after year, and, particularly, for marrying me to responsible representation.

Thanks to Terry Sanders, whose early encouragement was precisely the right ticket at exactly the right time; to Alex Ayres—to no small extent, this book is his fault, and God bless him for it; to a truly inspirational film faculty of another place and time: Irwin R. Blacker, Bernie Kantor, Arthur Knight, Dave Johnson, Mel Sloan, Doug Cox, Gene Peterson, Ken Miura, Dan Wiegand, Dick Harber, Herb Farmer, Wolfram VonHanwehr, and Herb Kosower; to Jim Henry and Allan Hollingsworth, world-class writers and computer mavens able to leap tall buildings in a single bound; to Kathy Anne Stumpe, for the names of the wildflowers; and to Lisa Gordon, for the bikes.

And finally, as always, love and gratitude to Pat, Susanna, and

Daniel for lending me that corner of the kitchen table (you can have it back now, but only for a moment) and for making life worth living.

Richard Walter
Los Angeles
November 1998

escape from film school

A NOVEL

FlashForward

I WISH I HAD DIED in some Hollywoody way: metal-on-the-highway, sex-drugs, murder-suicide.

The sorry truth is I choked to death on sushi.

The night was real and unreal, in too many ways just like a movie. The streets glistened in a halfhearted L.A. rain, as if slickened not by nature but a special-effects crew. In the distance a siren sang a dirge so mournful, so mellow as to suggest it, too, was exquisitely crafted artifice, digitally sweetened, dubbed, and Dolby'd into life's track during postproduction by a union cutter.

But an actual ambulance arrived and a flesh-and-blood pair of paramedics—an African American and an Asian—leaped from the doors and sprinted for the restaurant.

I lay facedown on the floor, quite thoroughly deceased now for some several minutes. The linoleum's coolness had welcomed and reassured me as my cheek settled upon it. Around me grouped diners, waiters, a chef, a tattooed white dishwasher who could only be a felon freshly furloughed from Folsom. In rapid-fire Japanese the owner scolded the dishwasher, driving him back into the kitchen just as the paramedics appeared in the doorway.

Ginger straddled me as she had only days earlier on the Indian cotton couch in my campus office. And even now, as she administered amateur CPR, her hazel eyes shone with the same bright panic that had informed her lovemaking. She pressed hard against my ribs, grunted and released, pressed, grunted, released.

What I required, of course, was not CPR but the Heimlich maneuver. Still, I forgive her. Ginger genuinely struggled to save me and I genuinely wanted to die.

Wedged in the restaurant's door frame like silent-film buffoons perpetually in each other's way, the paramedics feinted left and right, all the while scanning the premises as they struggled to extricate themselves. They popped free at last and dashed headlong for the booth where the small crowd around me had gathered. Recklessly sweeping Ginger aside in their haste, they caused her to smack her head smartly against the chrome table leg immediately across the narrow aisle.

Unnoticed in the attention visited now upon myself, Ginger entered a full-tilt swoon, deflating like a ruptured beach ball. Her eyes rolled back into her head and, off to the side, she settled into a cozy heap and lay perfectly still, limp as a rag doll, crumpled like a damp towel abandoned on a motel bathroom floor.

And now they were upon me, rotating my remains into the regulation anterior position. One pressed his ear hard against my chest, listening futilely for a heartbeat as the second administered expert—if pointless—resuscitation therapy. The first now readied the defibrillator.

The medic cranked up the rheostat to ten thousand volts. He grasped the metal shock plates' vinyl grips in either hand. But before he could order everybody clear, a patron noticed rich red blood trickling from Ginger's ear, charting a crooked course across her tawny California cheek.

And typically, even at my own death, Ginger upstaged me.

"This woman's hurt!" the customer shrieked.

Abandoning my still-warm corpse as quickly as they had pounced upon it, the paramedics ministered now to Ginger. Detecting a pulse, however feeble, they nodded in grim approval, then slipped the stretcher beneath her and hustled her all-perfect twenty-two-year-old form toward the door.

The onlookers flowed in the stretcher's wake toward the entrance and watched the men load Ginger into the wagon.

Lost and alone in the booth, my body steadily assuming room temperature, I lay quiet.

It seemed entirely appropriate that the final experience in my life had proved to be the rancid flavor of seared maguro—undercooked, overpriced tuna—lodged irrevocably in my windpipe.

It was all that I deserved.

1

LENNY BRUCE WAS DEAD.

That was the last thing we heard before the Blaupunkt blew, midway across the Penn Pike. Now, with no radio, Big Irish and I could do nothing to amuse ourselves but replicate Noo Yawk doowop sounds that were even then decrepit oldies.

We slept whenever fatigue overtook us, inflating air mattresses at roadside. The second night, along what still remained of 66, between Tulsa and Bartlesville, we gazed up at the Perseus showers and watched phosphorous meteors score the sky three, four, five times a minute, each and every one of them beckoning us to California.

Somewhere in the sea of grass west of Amarillo we appropriated a wonderfully preposterous moosehead coatrack that had been abandonded at roadside. We were able to maneuver it into the VW by standing it upright through the open canvas sunroof.

Irish, lunk that he was, had actually volunteered for the Marines only to come up 4-F—a bum knee. On the coast at last, I dropped him with family in Oxnard, where he figured to learn the lath-and-plaster dodge. Alone, I continued north in the rattling, buzzing Beetle to the Bay Area and observed real, true hippies.

Then, abruptly, I piloted the VW due south, altogether bypassing

L.A.'s mustard skyline, not stopping till Tijuana, where, just to be able to say I'd done it, wholly expecting to cluck my tongue in superior Anglo disapproval, I saw a bullfight. Instead, to my everlasting shame, I experienced transcendent awe through every blood-soaked veronica.

Finally, I drove back up the coast as far as Leo Carillo Beach and saw real, live surfers and also seals.

Wandering aimlessly on perilous roads through canyons, and on broad freeways where each individual lane rivaled whole eastern highways, I found myself at last somehow on Figueroa Street in the middle of what passed for downtown Los Angeles.

Across the street at Felix Chevrolet they were already advertising clearances to make room for the '67s. Broad posters covering the showroom windows boasted that GM would out-Mustang the Mustang with this thing called Camaro.

But I was a New York boy, and cars were transportation. It was 1966 and I did not think about cars, did not think about surfing, seals, hippies, bullfights. What I thought about was the war. What I thought about, more precisely, was the draft. And at long last I decided to turn myself in.

Two months had passed, maybe more, since I'd mailed my card back to Vincent Esposito, the clerk at the Queensboro Plaza Selective Service Center in Long Island City. I'd enfolded it in a Days of Rage rally flier upon the back of which was scrawled most respectfully my message: I would no longer play Good German to Lyndon Johnson's ego.

I had been on the lam now some sixty days. Having resolved to surrender, however, caused a strange serenity to settle over me.

I was not especially afraid to go to jail. Activist pals, Freedom Riders from the early civil rights days, told me they'd never had so much fun as when getting clapped into trashy county lockups. Boasts of such exploits, they assured me moreover, had encouraged firm-breasted, pointy-nippled, long-haired, faded-denim-clad women in artsy-craftsy-clinky-clanky earrings and no panties cavalierly to drop their bell-bottoms.

Peace movement counselors had assured me that after years of writs, waivers, motions, denials, dismissals, stipulations, petitions, and a potpourri of still other assorted processes and procedures, I'd eventually serve some fourteen months, tops, and at a federal honor farm on the order of Danbury or Lompoc, where I'd while away the hours puttering in the vegetable garden. And—though I could not yet appreciate it—if the timing was right, I'd even play knock-hockey in the rec room with high officials of the Nixon administration, including the Attorney General of the United States himself.

But this yawning, gaping calm was now suddenly lanced by the appearance in my mirror of a somehow familiar plain brown Buick sedan bearing U.S. government plates. Had it been tailing me for some distance?

Inside were two men—a Negro and an Oriental—wearing suits and ties. They drew alongside. In what was clearly a rehearsed motion, the black man at the passenger's window thrust his wallet at me vertically and let it fall open, exposing the gleaming bronze shape of a badge-sized shield.

"Federal marshals, son," he sang out quietly, almost an apology, in a basso to rival Levi Stubbs. Here was a practiced aw-shucks affect to soothe any fugitive's soul. Side by side we rolled to a stop at a light.

"Stuart Thomas," he continued, "please pull your vee-hickle to the curb. You are under arrest for violation of the Selective Service Act. You have the right to remain silent. In the event you choose to speak . . ."

I was vastly, overpoweringly relieved. I readied myself to pull to the curb, to step from the car, to offer up my wrists for shiny silver cuffs. I took a deep, cleansing breath and instructed myself not to panic.

At which point I promptly panicked.

Not waiting for the light to change, as if my flesh were not my own, as if my body were inhabited by an impostor, as if my right foot belonged to some stranger, as if I observed all this as a dispassionate party from across the street, I floored the pedal and lurched blindly through the impossibly heavy cross traffic at Adams Boulevard.

The Buick in hot pursuit, we careened down Figueroa. My four cylinders were no match for the oversized supercharged government-issue road machine, but in urban traffic my Volks provided something of an advantage.

A bus loomed up between us, followed by a Helms Bakery truck. I swerved left, right, this way, that, and found myself at last on a diminutive side street that was actually a service entrance to the campus of the University of Southern California. The chase ended as quickly as it had begun. The government sedan clearly had been trapped in traffic and was nowhere to be seen.

It was August and the quad was wholly deserted. The VW coughed to a halt at the end of a stunted street. My heart clicking like a ratchet, I abandoned the vehicle where it sat and raced into the nearest building, a ramshackle collection of interconnecting structures that appeared to be ancient wooden stables.

A crude plaque above the shabby entrance read: DEPARTMENT OF CINEMA.

A sign below it, hand-carved in polished mahogany, said: REALITY ENDS HERE.

2

the USC Cinema Department's floors—indoors
and out—were asphalt.

The plywood walls and ceilings were all a bilious gray-green beige.
No one with eyes in his head could have chosen such a hue; clearly
it represented a composite of short ends, the mix of remnants in
cans left over from other campus projects when the premises were
first painted early in the century.

I wandered aimlessly around this mismatched, disconnected collection of spaces. Here was a most unlikely venue for any center of
creative expression in any medium, much less the hotbed of talent
and discipline—the cutting edge of the sixties—for which it would
soon enough come to be celebrated all around the world.

Still, even now there was something seductive about the place.
The various decrepit structures surrounded a tidy, sunshine-
drenched, lush-green-grassy patio, and the contrast of darkness and
light was acutely appropriate to film. Corridors led this way and
that. Here, a crude soundstage. There, a classroom. Here, a funky,
comfy screening room. There, a bank of cramped, cluttered administrative offices. Here, an editing barn crammed with a dozen antique Moviolas plus a banner festooning the wall and proclaiming

every editor's desperate last hope: "The Music Will Carry It."

With the exception of my own anxious presence, every inch of the place appeared totally, spectacularly deserted.

Until the outer door flew open and the pair of panting federal marshals burst in. I ducked behind a square wooden column and moved around it in synch with the officers' own motion—this way, that way, not a little like Harpo—keeping the pillar between us. In this manner I remained invisible until without warning they darted through the open double doors of the dank, dark stage and altogether disappeared.

I seized the opportunity to prance through an open window into the administrative offices. I landed with a thud in the reception area, upsetting stacked reams of paper piled beside the mimeograph machine. I held my breath and hoped that the clatter had somehow escaped notice.

"In here, darling," a man's voice called softly. I looked toward the sound and saw the partly open door to an inner office. It bore a plastic nameplate: KEVIN BURNS, CHAIRMAN.

At this very moment the marshals reappeared from the sound-stage. I dropped to my hands and knees and crawled into the inner office, quietly kicking the door closed behind me.

"Veronica?" the same voice called, now closer, louder. I gazed straight ahead under the desk at a pair of knobby knees extending from loud Bermuda shorts and hairy, skinny calves with clown's feet shod in mismatched rubber thongs fresh from the bins at Pick'n'Save.

I sucked in a deep breath, and after a beat rose to find myself staring stupidly at a geeky, gawky mid-forties nerd. Had the word even been invented yet? Surely it was the only way to describe the guy with his greasy, curly black hair and beaky nose. Perched precariously about a mile down that nose were preposterous tortoiseshell half glasses secured by a too-ample string that drooped, looped, and ran around his neck. Gazing past stacks of books and pamphlets and papers and film cans hemming in and obscuring the desk, I could see that he wore a Hawaiian shirt. It featured what first appeared to be large black tarantulas but upon closer inspection were revealed to be broad, flat palm fronds against a Day-Glo electric canary sunset.

"We're not in session," Burns snapped. "Preregistration commences Monday."

That was fine with me. I nodded in silence and turned for the door, but as I cracked it just the littlest bit, I could make out the forms of the marshals emerging from the editing barn. I closed the door quietly and turned back to face Burns.

"Professor Burns?" I vamped. I had no earthly idea what I might say next.

"I'm not here," was Burns's overly even response.

"I've driven clear from New York just to see you," I said, surprising both myself and the chairman. Attempting to buy time, I reached across the desk and eagerly pumped his hand.

"You drove thousands of miles without bothering to make an appointment?" he said, retrieving his hand and inspecting it as if for damage. He looked up at me. "You're full of shit."

The door flew open and the marshals burst in.

"I am full of shit," I readily agreed, nodding morosely, "without a paddle." With the marshals' appearance I felt again vastly, overwhelmingly relieved. At last the jig was up. I would flee no farther. My newfound tranquillity was disturbed just slightly by unspoken questions, such as: Had resisting arrest blown my chances for the honor farm? Would I now be sent to Lexington or San Quentin? Instead of puttering in the veggie garden, would I be dicked up the ass by take-a-number cons awaiting their turn on long, long lines, as at a bakery?

One marshal snapped a bright chrome cuff on my wrist as the other informed me for the second time in ten minutes, "You have the right to remain silent . . ."

"That's a mixed metaphor," Kevin Burns said.

". . . in the event that you choose to speak . . ."

" 'Up shit's creek without a paddle,' " Burns explained.

". . . anything you say can . . ."

"Not 'full of shit without a paddle.' "

". . . and will be used against you . . ."

The second cuff snapped on my second wrist.

Now genuinely annoyed, Burns shifted his attention at last to the marshals. "This is a sacred scholarly sanctuary," he announced in a tone that was distinctly professorial.

". . . in a court of law."

"Did he knock over a bank?" Burns asked, rich with sarcasm, peering down his long nose first at one marshal, then panning to the other. "Did he gun down children in a schoolyard?"

Without replying, the marshals pivoted my body and prepared to escort me from the premises.

"Another draft case, right?" the chairman concluded. "This young man just happens to be one of our students."

The marshals paused. "Then why has he not filed for his 2-S classification?"

"I was just this red-hot minute completing his S.S. Form 109, Selective Service Student Deferment." Without looking down, Burns pulled a crisp, white, official-looking document from the seemingly hopeless mess of papers on his desk. He laid it out atop a flurry of bulletins and journals and seized a fat, old-fashioned fountain pen from a ceramic mug sporting an image of Southern Cal mascot Tommy Trojan bearing a sword, shield, and helmet and wearing a short pleated skirt.

I watched all of this as if it were a movie and had nothing whatever to do with my own true life.

"Last name first," Burns said.

I looked around the room awkwardly, not realizing that the person being addressed was myself.

"Last name first," Burns repeated dully, but at the same time there was no mistaking the irritation in his tone. He glared narrowly at me for a hefty moment.

But before I could state my last name first or, for that matter, say anything at all, a reedy, dusky voice called from the outer office, "Kev?"

The voice floated like fog from across a vast lake, and at the same time it sounded like a whisper close to my ear. Though its owner was not yet present, I swear I could feel her full, moist lips brush lightly against my lobe.

Chairman Kevin Burns winced as a radiant, heart-stopping strawberry-blond-hair-to-her-ass young beauty appeared in the doorway. She wore a long peasant skirt and a fluffy, puffy broad-collared flowery print blouse, open at the neck. It was not a particularly provocative outfit, especially for 1966 summertime Southern California, where a woman could be excused for tight, slit shorts and a loose, skimpy, stringy halter with no bra. On first glance—somehow even before first glance—I knew I would obsess about this creature every minute of every day for the rest of my life.

The federal officers, however, were singularly unimpressed by Veronica or anything else. They had a job to do, and they intended to do it.

Burns cleared his throat like a bad actor. "Miss Baldwin is another of our students," he informed the marshals as if they were even the least bit interested. "A doctoral candidate," he added in what was clearly an attempt merely to fill the painful, accusing silence. If the remark's substance failed to move them, its stammering, all-thumbs desperation certainly impressed me. Burns turned now to the woman herself. "I'll be with you in a moment, Veronica," he said, all business, and it was impossible for me not to wonder precisely what their business might be.

Sensing the awkwardness in the room, affecting a wide-eyed, lash-fluttering, brow-furrowing innocence, she explained to all present, "Professor Burns has consented to coach me for my orals."

3

thANKS, thEN, tO thE good offices of the University of Southern California's registrar, instead of slogging through the swamps of Southeast Asia or swabbing toilets at a federal corrections facility, I slept through boring foreign movies on the order of *Last Year at Marienbad.*

Meeting USC's exorbitant tuition—fifty dollars a credit—required no small scrimping. I cut overhead by combining transportation and housing: I lived in my car.

It wasn't so bad. Even with the moosehead coatrack, the VW bucket seats reclined enough to let me stretch out. If I could not exactly sleep, I could catnap. The hardest part was rising every hour to plunk another dime in the meter.

To earn those dimes, to cover that tuition, I found part-time employment in the food trades. Specifically, I slung tacos at La Reina de Los Burritos on Vermont near Exposition, in the university district. Not only could I earn over a buck an hour, I could scarf all the beans I could refry.

All things considered, my life was splendidly, perhaps even perfectly arranged. I was far from the Mekong Delta. I had room, board, job. And if film school was merely an elaborate draft dodge, I found myself actually enjoying the classes, even if doing so required an occasional smidgen of cocky sophomoric cynicism.

I recall, for example, my professor patiently explaining the merits of *Marienbad* (which we students covertly designated *Marienworse*). "In the film," he asserted, "Resnais integrates Panofsky's paradigm: the spatialization of time and the dynamization of space." He paused to let it all sink in. "And it has a secondary status," he continued after a moment, "in that its supplementarity acknowledges post modern structure even as it reveals the ethnocentric roots of old world metaphysics."

Students stretched and yawned with luxurious abandon.

Inexplicably, however, I found myself deeply, darkly depressed. Student status entitled me to the university's free medical services, and eventually I found the strength to flee to the campus shrink. "What you need," he told me, "is group therapy." And that was just about the last time I heard his voice, though he supervised our sessions, week after week after week, physically present in the room, but always exuding a well-trained Freudian silence.

"Of course you're depressed," scolded a member of the group in the first session, a close-cropped fellow from Bakersfield with a fogbound gaze. "You're shirking your responsibility to your country. How do you expect to feel? The nation calls, and what is your response? A jackpot, giveaway, draft-dodge degree in some Mickey Mouse discipline like movies that doesn't even belong in a self-respecting institution of higher learning."

"Or here at USC," another fellow quipped. He wore ragged army surplus togs and ratty shoulder-length hair bound in a scarlet headband.

"Want to feel good?" Crew Cut glared at me, demanding an answer. I remained silent. "Do your duty," he said at last. "Take up arms. The hour is late. If we don't stop the Commies in Asia today, they'll storm the freaking border at Nogales tomorrow."

"And if not tomorrow," Headband said, "Saturday, the latest."

"It's easier to crack cheap jokes," Crew Cut replied, "than to take responsibility for yourself and for your nation."

"Where's your own responsibility for the nation?" Headband shot back.

Crew Cut looked sadly at the floor. He choked, swallowed hard. "I'm 4-F. Bad ankle." He paused dramatically. "An accident. Water skiing." He raked the room with his half-dead gaze. "It's still a struggle for me even to walk, for Christ's sake," he said, rising to his feet, hobbling a few steps around the room, then returning to his chair and easing himself down into it. "Hey, I could have drowned. Don't look at me like that," he pleaded. "I support our boys in Vietnam."

"I support our boys in Vietnam, too," I heard a voice say, and realized it was my own. "It's the boys in Washington I don't support. The war's a mistake. I want what the boys want: bring them home. Today. Better, yesterday."

"And if not yesterday," the kid in the army surplus garb piped up, "Saturday, the latest." He looked me in the eye, shifted in his seat. "Instead of sitting around intellectualizing," he said, "take action. Get relevant, brother. Bomb the goddamned ROTC. Kill a cop."

"I like cops," I quietly confessed.

"Fine," he said, dismissing me, tossing back his locks in a gesture that was meant to appear casual and natural but clearly had been practiced repeatedly before a mirror.

"Then flee to Canada," said another kid, shrugging.

"What's so great about Canada?" I asked. "I happen to love my country." I turned back to the guy with the headband. "What about you?" I asked him. "Why don't you do something?"

He looked down at the floor. "I'm 4-F," he mumbled. "Bad ankle." He looked up at the group. "I hurt it in a riot at a Strawberry Alarm Clock concert." When the group failed to respond, he became indignant and self-righteous. "Hey, I was nearly trampled. Don't look at me like that," he said again. "I've written to both senators," he said.

Now an anemic, barefoot wispy young woman with bad skin spoke up suddenly, blowing away the curtain of hair hanging in front of her face. Looking deeply into my eyes, she said, "We're not here to discuss ideology." She turned to the psychiatrist for approval, but he did not react in any discernible way. She swiveled to face me. "You're depressed," she said breathily, "because you're a film student, an artist. And art is for feeling and artists feel their feelings passionately."

"I'm an artist, all right," I told her, nodding. "A bullshit artist."

To my astonishment, the shrink now looked up and leaned forward in his chair. It was clear that he was actually going to speak. I could not imagine what he might say, but I was also wholly confident it would represent a timeless, life-changing insight that would forever set me right, that would liberate me perpetually from the various arbitrary wrong turns of my earliest days, that would provide newfound and eternal serenity.

"We have to stop now," he said. "That's all the time we have for today."

4

the DAYS DRAGGED ON and, in eloquent testimony to my deepening depression, my primary activity was no activity at all.

Mainly, I slept.

I slept in my car. I slept in my classes. I slept behind the grill at La Reina de Los Burritos taco stand on South Vermont Avenue where, in a daze one afternoon, I was mindlessly ladling lard when a familiar voice sang out, "A dozen tacos."

I looked up into the hauntingly beautiful eyes of Veronica Baldwin. I saw her from time to time in and around the cinema department, but forever averted my gaze. Surely she could tell simply by looking at me that she owned me totally and forever—as, say, the United States owned the Panama Canal. How could she not appreciate that I would here and now waltz directly into traffic on Exposition Boulevard and lie facedown on the pavement if only she'd hint that the act would provide her even a moment's amusement?

"Stuart!" she gasped. "You work here?"

"The hours are long," I conceded, "but the pay's lousy." I waited for a giggle but was met instead by a curious stare. "I eat for free," I added defensively.

"Eat what?" she said, wrinkling her nose in disapproval, gesturing toward the greasy, festering taco fillings. "That poison?"

"Poison?" I said. "You just ordered a dozen of the little buggers."

"Not for myself," she said. "Cast and crew. I'm catering a shoot. Student film project 480," she explained, referring to the course's designation in the USC catalog. "Call it a cinematic tone poem, an exploration, a celebration of human spirituality, physicality, consciousness, and context. It examines certain central questions relating to the nexus between visual experiential phenomena and creativity."

"It sounds fascinating," I lied. What in the world she was talking about?

"Join us!" she said suddenly. "I'm desperate for a guy to work the boom."

I checked my watch. "Got another hour here," I said at the same time as I prepared Veronica's order.

"You should lose this joint," she said, grimly regarding the food stand. "Apply to the student aid office for financial assistance. There are internships, scholarships, fellowships, and those are just the -ships. Ask Kev—Professor Burns—to write you a letter of reference."

"The chairman? Never. He's been far too generous to me already."

"Generous?" she said. "Kevin?"

"Saved my ass from the draft," I explained, although it was hardly necessary; had not Veronica witnessed the action that crazy afternoon only some handful of weeks ago? "It's just his small way," I speculated, "of opposing the war."

"He supports the war," she said. "He needed your ass for the cinema program."

"And what good's my ass to the cinema program?"

"You think Vietnam's the only place for body counts?" she asked. "They count bodies right here on campus. It's called enrollment. It's not easy to get people to commit time and tuition to a fringe discipline like movies."

"But doesn't it lead to employment in the motion picture business?"

"Sure it does." She nodded. "With perseverance and influence—and a tuxedo—you might eventually land a slot as an usher."

I finished preparing her final taco, wrapped it and stuffed it along with the others into a bag, and shoved them across the counter to the girl of my dreams. "I slipped you some extra hot sauce," I told her.

"Extra hot sauce!" she exclaimed brightly. "That's brilliant!"

"It is?" I said, feeling perhaps just a bit—maybe more than just a bit—patronized.

"Absolutely!" she insisted, smiling through the smog. She shoved a bill at me and, not waiting for change, seized the big bag of tacos and turned to leave. "Extra hot sauce!" she said again. "Why, it's a breakthrough!" She headed for her car.

I knew not what in the world she meant, but it was clear that I had pleased her. A glow settled over me, and I knew that to please Veronica was to please myself. I pressed her bill to my face and sniffed it for the lingering scent of her long, graceful fingers' natural oils. I studied the bill carefully, half expecting ol' Abe to break out into a big, broad grin. In the next moment, however, it dawned on me that five bucks would not cover the tab. Instead of shorting the register, which would have been as easy as buttoning my shirt, with glee I made up the missing three dollars and thirty-seven cents from my own pocket.

5

NOT TWENTY MINUTES lATER, at the same time as I was scraping grease from the grill with a spatula during my afternoon's final hour at the taco joint, on the film school's soundstage a feminine hand erased the words "Student Film Project 480" and, clutching a fat piece of chalk, inscribed the legend "Extra Hot Sauce."

Veronica Baldwin regarded the slate and nodded with satisfaction. "Roll," she called at last.

"Speed," said cameraman Slade Sloan, a charming, smooth-skinned, coffee-colored soul in his early twenties.

Veronica clapped together the zebra-striped sticks mounted atop the slate, producing a crisp slap, like a flat hand spanking a full, round butt. With a flourish, like a matador wielding his cape, she whisked it away from the lens.

A half-dozen students—her crew—stood around a brightly lit pair of young actors, one male, one female, both naked. Veronica ordered, "Action!" On cue, the two slammed their bodies together. And right there on the asphalt floor they writhed and wriggled and wound themselves into a glistening fleshy knot.

So here was Veronica's cinematic tone poem, her exploration, her celebration of human spirituality, physicality, consciousness, and context and whatever else she had said at the taco stand. Truth to tell, had I been there it would have struck me as a lot of fucking and sucking, not so much film form as film fornication.

Without taking her eyes off the tangle of heads, limbs, torsos, hair, and assorted orifices, Veronica leaned over to Slade. Barely moving her lips, she inquired under her breath, "How's it look?"

"Soft," her cameraman replied, shaking his head slightly, not removing his eye from the eyepiece's supple rubber cup.

But as quietly as he pronounced it, and notwithstanding the cranking ratchet whir of the unblimped 16mm Arriflex motor, the comment was overheard by the male player. "Soft?" he said, disentangling himself from his companion and looking up at the crew.

"Cut," Veronica told Slade Sloan, annoyed. He shut off the Arri. She reprimanded the actor. "You don't stop until I say 'Cut.'"

"You just said 'Cut,'" the actress called from the floor, where she lay on her back, her hands behind her head. Trying to get comfortable, she rolled over onto her side, propped herself on an elbow, drew one leg up against her body so that the knee came to rest against her breast. From this curious vantage she watched the events as if she were an impartial observer, as if she were fully clothed instead of jaybird naked on the cold, hard floor.

"That was because he stopped acting," Veronica explained with poorly simulated patience.

"Soft?" the actor said again, incredulous, outraged. "Soft?" Shameless, he looked down at his stiff and swollen member. The shaft bobbed and dipped deeply as he moved his body even just slightly. The organ was so rigid, so erect as to lend it a curve and swoop and arch, its circumcised mushroom tip finally peering back at its owner and practically kissing his belly button.

"He's talking about the focus," Veronica explained. She turned back to Slade. "Why soft?"

"Cheap lens," he said. "Mistreated by too many amateur crews."

"Just be sure to catch the climax," Veronica instructed her cameraman. She turned back to the actor. "Let us know when you're ready."

"I'm ready," he said urgently. "I'm ready."

"Hang on one second, can you?" Veronica requested.

It was at precisely this moment that I entered the soundstage. I admit I was astonished to see the sleek, gleaming bodies lolling casually about the place. Moreover, I found the all-business demeanor of the players distinctly arousing. Their casual, no-big-deal attitude provided so bold a contrast to the brazen sexuality as to enhance its eroticism exponentially. Holding my breath, struggling to project the ho-hum affect displayed by the others present, I hung back quietly in the entrance to the stage and gaped.

Veronica turned back to Slade Sloan. "Pan left and zoom in as tight as you can, okay? As close as you can on the penetration, got it?"

Slade nodded. "A single on the dingle," he said.

"Roll," said Veronica.

"Speed."

"Action."

"What about the clapper?" Slade Sloan asked, not removing his eyes from the lens.

"Fuck the clapper," Veronica said. "There's so much camera noise we'll have to dub the grunts and groans during post." She turned to the girl. "Are you still moist, honey?" Veronica's tone was strictly clinical. "Need a squeeze of jelly?" Observing all this, I wondered if it wasn't all some sweet, sweaty hallucination.

"I don't need no jelly, Cry-sakes," the girl said.

"Fine." Veronica nodded. "Let your knees fall apart, okay?"

"What's my motivation?"

"You're horny and you want to get laid," Veronica explained.

The young woman lay back and performed as instructed.

"Great," Veronica said. "I appreciate that." She turned to the male. "Can you penetrate for us now, can you?"

He got down on the floor once again and positioned himself atop the woman. He tried at first to insert his organ by maneuvering his hips and thighs, thrusting, poking, but it was all to no avail. Finally he reached down, seized his penis with his fingers and guided it to his partner. Its head met the first set of lips, resisted for a second, and even bent just a bit. The young woman moaned; she seemed to be attempting to convey pleasure, but to me it sounded like pain.

And now the tip suddenly popped through and slid smoothly among parting flesh curtains, past all the various folds of soft, damp skin. The man gasped, the woman groaned, and I, myself, from my vantage at the door, involuntarily moaned and then, catching myself, choked. Embarrassed, I quickly scanned the scene and was pleased to note that, thanks to the Arri's cranky movement, nobody had heard my own vocalizing.

"Great!" Veronica said. "Okay, are you ready? Can you do, it?"

"I can do it," he gasped. "I can do it."

"Excellent," Veronica said. "Now hump just a little bit, in, out, that's right, bump, grind till you're really, really ready."

"I'm really, really ready."

"Are you going to spurt?"

"Yeah. Yeah."

"Good. Yank it out now and give us a regular gusher." From her flat, everyday tone she might have been ordering a sandwich at a lunch counter.

"I'm ready," the young man said. "Here we go."

But from the camera there now arose a sudden new noise, a fluttering, as if cards were being endlessly shuffled. "Hold it!" Slade Sloan cried out. "Camera jam!"

"Here I come!" the actor said. "Gusher!"

"No!" Veronica said. "Wait!"

"Can't help it! Too late!" He withdrew from the girl and knelt between her legs. His penis nodded over her abdomen like one of those bobbing trinkets Stuart had seen mounted to the rear shelves of cars on the east side of town.

"No!" Veronica shouted.

Even from my own position afar back in the shadows beyond the crew's perimeter I could see the milky gray fluid fly. It sprayed all over the female's belly and breasts. She lifted her head to watch and a pale, cloudy globule caught her smack in the eye. Instead of re-treating, she struggled to slide her body down between her partner's thighs, as if to get her mouth in position to engulf his scrotum. As she did so, a stray drop of semen landed on a brightly glaring 10K bulb, a so-called kicker positioned just above and behind the players, providing a stark, raw backlight. With a sharp, crackling hiss it fried itself to paste, then to dust. The noise recalled for me the grill sizzling at La Reina de Los Burritos taco stand.

"No!" Veronica insisted, but there was nothing to do about it now. The actor shuddered and panted and sank back onto the mat-tress, trembling, exhausted.

Veronica turned to Slade. "Did you get it? Did you?"

Slade pessimistically regarded his camera. He ran the grumpy motor forward for several seconds. Now he unlatched the small black door in the Arri's side. An accordion of jammed footage sprung from the camera like a jack-in-the-box, not a little reminiscent of the actor's spraying semen. All that was missing was the Jew's-harp-twanging *boing!* of a Saturday-morning kids' cartoon.

Clearly the footage was useless. "It's these damned German movements," Slade explained, woefully inspecting the camera's innards. He fiddled with this and that, then hand-cranked the movement forward some several frames, pulling out bits of torn celluloid. Now he reloaded the film into the teeth and raced the motor forward to verify that the loop would hold.

Marginally satisfied, he snapped shut the camera door and nodded to Veronica.

"All right." Veronica sighed. "We'll try it again."

"Again?" the actor asked, furious. "Again?" He scooped up a bathrobe from where it lay nearby across a steel folding chair, wrapped it around himself, and stormed directly past me through the soundstage door and into the still-bright Southern California daylight.

Watching the actor's departure, Veronica for the first time noticed my presence. "Still need a guy to work the boom?" I inquired lamely, in a tone that was decidedly hoarse.

Veronica stared at me through narrowing eyes, as if appraising me at auction. She turned to Slade. The two looked at each other, then back at me, but neither spoke. Finally Slade turned back to Veronica and shrugged. Veronica studied me for another long moment. "Ever done any acting?" she asked.

The young woman still naked on the floor now rose abruptly. She, too, draped a robe over her shoulders. "Forget it," she said. "I don't ball just anybody who walks in off the street. I'm an artist. I have to find my center. I have to emote." And she, too, swept past me and out the door.

Veronica remained quite perfectly calm. And now, with monumental nonchalance, she began quietly and methodically unbuttoning her own blouse.

6

THERE ARE THINGS I do not do.

I do not, for example, bare my butt in front of a group of people, to say nothing of strangers, never mind a camera. I'm no actor, and I am a bit of a prude.

So instead of stripping off my own clothes, instead of rolling around on the floor with Veronica wrapped in nothing but each other's arms, I stood fully dressed above her and operated the clumsy, clunky, unblimped 16mm Arriflex and watched her roll around naked on the floor with black, bare-assed Slade Sloan.

I watched them combine and couple every which way—front, back, top, bottom, upside down, downside up, coiling 'round and 'round each other, squirming, slithering like serpents. Notwithstanding my poker face, I was positively frantic with lust. Frankly, I experienced a jealous rage that was pathological.

I distracted myself by racking focus, panning, tilting, zooming, and following the action only through the lens, pretending it was occurring trillions of light years from here. And I distracted myself also by contemplating the fact that these activities—the amateur filming of an amateur sucking-and-fucking extravaganza—were deemed by the Pentagon to be so essential to our nation's defense as to warrant my dispensation from the carnage in Southeast Asia; a darker brother could take my place there too, as Slade did here and now.

The war came home before the boys did and swirled all around us, with body bags tallied nightly on the news as if merely an extension of the sports wrap-up. At staid, steady, sunshiny USC, Vietnam's impact was remarkably unremarkable. The lone protest involved the appearance of the Yippie Jerry Rubin, who, like the militant black radical Eldridge Cleaver, eventually ended up selling pants.

"Fuck Ronnie Reagan!" Rubin shouted in the one and only antiwar demonstration tolerated on our campus. It was still an era when people could provoke excitement merely by talking dirty in public. "Fuck Ronnie Reagan! Come on! Everybody! Fuck Ronnie Reagan! Fuck . . ." And soon enough the crowd was chanting, but with barely a fraction of the enthusiasm manifested at a Beat the Bruins football rally several days earlier.

Whatever the war in Vietnam had to do with the new governor of California—himself clearly a flash in the pan, a brief bit of right-wing West Coast guerrilla theater—escaped me. Did anybody doubt he'd so disgrace and humiliate himself as to retire after a single term and fade into richly merited obscurity?

Somebody tossed a rainbow-colored pharmaceutical capsule at the stage. The scuffy, grubby Rubin, bobbing like a trained seal, caught it in his mouth and downed it with a hard, dry swallow. Surely if the FBI or CIA or NSC or LAPD or anybody else wanted to off this dude, they had merely to station an undercover freak at the next demonstration, and have him toss a multihued capsule laced with strychnine.

Myself, I escaped the war's horror and evaded its issues in film classes, in slinging tacos, in my sweet-and-sour obsession with Veronica Baldwin, particularly in supporting her efforts to complete Student Film Project 480. Gradually I found myself taking over more and more aspects of the production. Was she foisting the responsibility for the picture upon me? That was okay. It was a distraction from my general ennui, the darkness that came constantly to color my mood. But best of all, it linked me ever more irrevocably with Veronica.

In the midst of worldwide turmoil, therefore, I shuffled lackadaisically through the motions of the starving student's life. The lighting instructor taught me the difference between a reflective and a direct reading. The editing teacher taught me the difference between code and edge numbers, between printer's and editor's synch. The sound instructor showed me how to mike the Doors. Jim and the boys themselves, then film students not at 'SC but UCLA, had come over to try out the school's crude sound recording facility. My impression of Morrison was that he was a fourth-rate impression of Jagger's fifth-rate impression of oppressed black American blues artists.

Most significantly, however, the writing teacher taught me how to pitch.

I sat among a dozen students around a long, rectangular table at the head of which was Gordon Michaels, a screenwriter I had never heard of. Of course, back then, there was not a single screenwriter—not one—I or anyone beyond the industry had ever heard of. It was not that there were no great screenwriters—quite the contrary; it was merely that none had ever been heard of. Screenwriters wrote; they were not written about.

Michaels was a paunchy, bedraggled eccentric, a social cripple, under whose gruff, belching, farting veneer resided a vulgarian's soul.

"Let's go around the table," he growled at the first meeting. "Pitch to the class a brief overview of the script you'll write."

His face went suddenly pale. He grimaced, clutched his chest. The class sat there, breathless as the instructor fumbled in his vest pocket and produced a pillbox from which he extracted a tiny white tablet. He placed it under his tongue. After a moment he relaxed. At last he nodded at the student on his right.

"A guy and a gal," the student said dutifully, "go thumb-tripping across America."

Michaels nodded at the next student, an ebony youngster dressed in a flowing orange dashiki. "The black experience. The man puts the slam on my main man and slams the man in the slammer."

Michaels panned only his eyeballs to the next student, who said perfunctorily, "Sex, drugs, rock, roll."

It was the fourth student's turn. "Some kids go hitch-hiking across America."

"Sand, surf, girls," said the next student.

"My story," said the next in line around the table, a fellow actually wearing a sport coat, even if his shirt was open at the collar and his tie rolled up and stuffed in his pocket, "succinctly replicates the profile of product currently being acquired by the new management at Warner Brothers–Seven Arts."

The next student said: "Sucking, fucking, humping." After a moment he elaborated: "Whips, chains, blow jobs, whatever." And after yet another pause he added: "A love story."

A pale, skinny woman with long, unkempt hair rasped, "A woman seeks to define her space, her place. She attempts to identify her perimeters, her parameters, her strictures, her structures."

Another student hesitated, then grunted, "Hitchhiking. America."

And at last it was my own turn. All eyes were upon me. I had no earthly idea what in the world I would write. And I had, therefore, no earthly idea what in the world I would say. At long last I heard myself assert, "I'm going to write something, anything . . . that's not boring."

Along with everyone else in the class I looked at Professor Gordon Michaels. With both hands he gripped the table. Dramatically, he now removed his right hand from the table and used it to massage his left shoulder. He furrowed his brow and struck a What-me-worry? pose but seemed at the same time clearly distressed. He popped another small white pill under his tongue.

And at last he spoke. "Class dismissed."

7

ON the SMALL, PALE, flickering greenish screen of the crude Moviescope viewer resting awkwardly in my lap—its power cord plugged into an adapter and then into my Volkswagen's cigarette lighter—Slade Sloan and Veronica Baldwin gobbled each other's faces and humped and bumped and ground their naked bodies together over and over and over again. Hand-cranking the rewinds forward and back, I derived a perverse glee in the control over their lovemaking that film technology afforded me.

Occasionally one or the other's mouth opened in a here-silent gasp or moan. I thought I recalled the precise accompanying sounds they'd made when I'd photographed the scene, but I wondered also whether I wasn't merely projecting my own lust, my own passion.

When here and now I heard Veronica's actual voice I was startled. First, no track had been recorded during this part of the shoot. Moreover, even if sound had been recorded, there was no playback connected to the Moviescope. Nevertheless, crisply and directly, in her ultra-fine-grain sandpaper rasp, Veronica said plain as day: "I didn't realize 909 West Thirtieth was your car."

I stared in disbelief at the now-frozen on-screen image of the tip of Slade Sloan's engorged, uncircumcised, eggplant-purple penis grazing Veronica's full, meaty lips. "Stuart? Stuart?" she asked, the lips remaining perfectly still.

There was the sound of knuckles rapping on safety glass.

I turned to see Veronica standing there in the street beside the car, bending forward awkwardly so that she could speak to me through the closed window. For a generous moment I lost myself in the depths of her unspeakably beautiful eyes, then involuntarily dropped my gaze to the open top two buttons of her cranberry raw-silk blouse.

She could see plain as day where my attention was directed, but somewhat in defiance, and perhaps partly also as a seduction, she maintained her rock-steady pose. This afforded me a clear vision of the creamy sweet whiteness of her smallish breasts, the chestnut nipples not quite stiff, not quite soft. They did not exactly jiggle but more precisely trembled in sympathy with her words as she spoke them, in a way like an audio VU meter formed from female flesh, the needle bobbing, quivering.

"This is where you're cutting my picture?" she called through the glass.

"The editing barn's completely booked," I explained, rolling down the window. I stared at Veronica just a little too long. I caught my breath and asked, "Did you bring the main title?"

"Fresh from the lab," she said, producing a spool of film wound on a canary-yellow plastic core. Upon a length of white pressure-sensitive tape, in red editor's grease pencil, there was scrawled the legend "Extra Hot Sauce."

I began rewinding the reel. "Is it cutting together?" she asked me.

"The splices are holding," I said.

"You know that's not what I mean. Does it contain its own internal film logic? Does it make any sense?"

"One sense," I told her. "Smell."

I reached the beginning of the reel and began splicing the newly delivered title footage to the head. As I fit the film into the splicer, I sliced a piece of clear, double-sprocketed Mylar from the roll, and Veronica said, "You're being negative."

"Negative?" I said, indicating the footage. "This is no negative. This is a fine-grain interpositive dupe off the camera original, a work print."

Veronica looked at me for a long moment. "You're pissed," she said at last, almost shyly, shaking her head slowly and looking down at the pavement. "You're pissed because I posed on-screen without panties."

"What're your panties to me?" I asked. "What's it to me what you do with your panties?"

"Stuart Thomas," she said, looking directly at me, "there is not now, nor has there ever been, anything between me and Slade Sloan."

"You're free to do whatever you wish with whoever you want without explanations to me," I said, cavalierly tossing my head. I feared the motion came across as a kind of palsy, a tic.

"The sex was mechanical," she insisted. "This is film. It's pretense."

I gestured toward the Moviescope screen. "You merely pretend to swap spit with Slade, to scarf down his schlong and squat on his face and ride his pole all greasy with your sweetly stinking juices?" My outburst shocked not only Veronica but also myself. Was misogynistic vulgarity the way to win the girl of one's dreams? I realized I'd lost all sense of decorum, and much more than merely that. I seriously wondered whether I wouldn't have been better off having surrendered to the military marshals in the first place, cooling my heels in some federal corrections facility, working off my draft dodge manufacturing license plates.

"The sex is real in only the most technical sense," Veronica replied after a moment. "The emotions are fake. My only chance is to win a slot on the artsy-craftsy student film festival circuit. The judges are all men. Men want to see skin. So I put some skin in the picture. Okay, it wasn't intended to be my own skin, but you were there, you saw what happened. You gotta go with the flow, right?"

Was this logic or illogic that Veronica spoke? I felt as if I no longer knew up from down, left from right, inside from outside.

"I can also merchandise the footage to the nudie-cutie market," Veronica continued. "They can run pornography and call it film artistry." Her arguments seemed all at once preposterous and sensible.

"Look," she said, "Slade's a nice enough guy, and a capable cameraman with a good eye. But otherwise he means nothing to me. Hey, it's showbiz." When I did not respond, she added quietly, demurely, fluttering her natural four-inch lashes, "It could have been you. You turned me down."

"Why are you telling me this?" I said, looking up from my splicing. "Screw the chairman if it suits you. Screw Slade Sloan for the sake of showbiz. But if there's nothing between you, how come you live together?" I returned to the splice, applied the Mylar, and all too vigorously commenced cranking the rewind.

"Live together? We cut costs splitting the rent. Not just Slade and me, but also two other guys. Hey, all three of them—Slade included—are gay."

"Gay?"

"That's what homosexuals want to be called now. Actually, Slade wants to be called bisexual, that's what he considers himself to be. Personally, I believe a bisexual is a gay person in denial." Veronica paused as if to let all this information sink in, but my head was swimming with both confusion and the musky sweet aroma of her hair and her breath.

She paused now for a hefty moment, looking me directly in the eye. Her voice now dropped to a nearly imperceptible whisper. "I like you, Stuart. I like you a lot. I was so impressed with the pluck you demonstrated that first day when you outfoxed the draft cops. And I'm enormously taken with the way you've asserted yourself creatively, virtually taking over my whole movie."

Had I taken over her movie or had it taken over me? Had I asserted myself, or had she seduced me into doing all the heavy cleaning? From the chance encounter at the taco stand that had led directly to my manning the boom at the shoot, I had been coaxed into synching dailies (marrying dialogue to image) and now into editing the entire movie. Was I subtly worming my way into Veronica's production in an attempt—conscious or not—to get closer to her? Or was Veronica simply exploiting me in the service of her own narrow purpose?

Ever more swiftly powering the rewind, I gestured toward the automobile interior. "My lease on this place runs another year." And at precisely this point the crank snapped off in my hand and footage went flying in elegant elliptical arcs all over the VW.

"You are jealous," Veronica observed quietly. She seemed to say it as much to herself as to me.

And just now my antique alarm clock pealed. I extricated myself from beneath the rewind and viewer, leaned forward to the passenger door, and flipped the handle forward. I opened the door, stepped to the pavement, and plunked another dime in the parking meter.

"Who're you kidding?" Veronica said, observing my little ritual. "This patch of pavement runs you ten cents an hour, that's two-forty a day, better than—what?—seventy bucks a month. You could get a comfy, cozy corner of our humble cottage for less than half that." She folded her arms and regarded me curiously. "With indoor plumbing," she added.

"It's out of the question," I said, not looking up. I avoided her gaze by fumbling with the meter, and when I'd milked that beyond reason I returned to the car, pulled out the rewind, and distracted myself toying with its gears, attempting to insert the slipped crank into its gnarled and toothy steel fitting.

"And I don't screw the chairman," Veronica said, just a little self-righteously. "An occasional dry hump, maybe. Okay, a hand job once. Once! It's a whole lot less degrading than waitressing."

In silence I continued to pretend to ignore her, flailing at the rewind with the detached crank. She hesitated another moment, as if awaiting a response. Finally she added, "Or slinging tacos."

8

except for the hills, real Hollywood does not look a bit like reel Hollywood. And no section diverges more widely from outsiders' romanticized expectations than commercial-industrial-warehouse Hollywood—above and below Santa Monica Boulevard—where Slade Sloan now piloted his beat-up old Chevy Greenbrier van.

He parked in the yellow zone fronting C&B Feco on North Citrus, jumped down from the driver's perch, sprinted around front, and met me as I descended from the passenger side. I took one end of the board on which the rewinds were mounted, and he took the other. Like Polanski's two men struggling with the wardrobe, together we made our way to the equipment-repair facility at the rear.

The usual early-morning broken-equipment panic raged full tilt, with unit managers and production supervisors pleading for special attention, attempting to get this or that patched, to replace one or another piece of recalcitrant gear that was holding up their shoot, squandering thousands and thousands of dollars every hour. We maneuvered our way to the counter and plunked down the rewinds before a distracted khaki-jacketed clerk. "Replace the crank pinion," Slade called over his shoulder, "and put it on the USC account."

We were halfway to the door when the clerk sang out, "Wait up. The KEM flatbed's ready."

Slade and I looked at each other, and then we looked back at the clerk. "KEM flatbed?" Slade asked.

The clerk drew a slip from a shallow drawer beneath the counter and peered at it closely. "Restored the pivot arm rotor," he said, "plus the number two track sprocket drive."

When we continued to stare at him in silence, the man said, "UCLA, right? Didn't you say you're from UCLA?"

Granted, it was easy enough to confuse USC and UCLA. Even my own dear mother perpetually misinformed people that I was a student at UCLA, and why not? The institution with "L.A." in its title was not in L.A. but in Westwood. That without "L.A." was smack dab in the center of L.A. The closest Mom would ever get to the truth was occasionally to pronounce "USCLA."

Ironically, years later, long after I had departed 'SC and formed an association instead with UCLA, Mom had finally straightened it out and perpetually misinformed people that I was associated now with USC. Perhaps it was because my classmates of that era had achieved substantial acclaim, coming virtually to own Hollywood, except for one who would soon enough come to own Marin County up north, just across the bridge from San Francisco.

But part of Mom's allure is that she has always been charmingly out of synch by perhaps ten frames with just about all of God's creation.

"Didn't you say you're from UCLA?" the clerk asked us again.

"Actually," I began, "we're from—" but Slade cut me off.

"UCLA. Right," he affirmed, nodding vigorously, turning to me and screwing up his face, indicating to me that I should clamp it. "UCLA," he said again. "How about that Alcindor!"

The satisfied clerk scanned the paperwork more closely. "Also got the 16 Mitchell Reflex S-SR plus two Nagra synch-pulse sound re-corders." Satisfied, he looked up and thrust the papers at me. "Dot-ted line," he said.

I stared at the document. "Sign it," Slade ordered.

The clerk was momentarily distracted by another customer and while he looked away I whispered to Slade through the side of my mouth, "Not me. I sign nothing."

"Go ahead," Slade insisted.

I shook my head.

"Sign," Slade said impatiently. "It's no big deal."

"If it's no big deal," I said, "why don't you sign?"

"Fine," Slade said, nodding. He seized the form and scrawled a signature. I had no idea, of course, that the name he signed was my own; that information would be made part of the public record all too soon. For now we found ourselves at the loading dock cramming the van with perhaps seventy-five thousand Lyndon Johnson dollars' worth of purloined equipment, courtesy of our esteemed and be-loved crosstown rival.

9

the "humble cottage" veronica Baldwin had
told me about is now the number three southbound lane of the
Glendale Freeway below La Cañada–Flintridge. Back then, however,
it was an authentic mansion.

From the massive sunken living room, one gazed through panoramic windows at the serene, snowcapped San Gabriels. Craning
your neck just a little provided a view—if the Santa Ana blew—of
the sparkling Pacific in the far, far distance. Indeed, on an extraordinarily clear day you could witness even the low shoulder of Cat-
alina breaching the surf some twenty-six miles across the sea.

The digs were sufficiently spacious to enable myself and my roommates—Veronica, Slade, and two other film students, Perry and
Troy—each to have our own ample bedroom and bath. Slade, Perry,
and Troy, however, shared the sprawling master suite, and why not?
The chamber was so big that you could fly a plane in it; the bed
was so vast the plane could land on it. Why couldn't three guys
comfortably sleep in it?

With the three sharing, it was possible not only for Veronica to
have her own room but for me and my moosehead coatrack to have
not one but two bedrooms, adjoining. I slept in the first and con-

verted the second into an editing suite. Here, then, was the "comfy, cozy corner" Veronica had promised me.

She had told me there was indoor plumbing, but had not mentioned that there was outdoor plumbing, too: a gorgeous turquoise pool fed by a waterfall. Even the bed I slept in was water. Water beds were all the rage, representing the latest in sleep engineering technology. It was enormously comfortable, but attempting to sleep in it produced in me also a queasy sensation. I solved my problem by popping a Dramamine at bedtime the way some of our film school pals were now regularly popping other kinds of pills. As in Hollywood, stuff that was smoked was giving way to stuff that was snorted or swallowed: uppers, downers, and in-betweeners.

Here I was, a starving, struggling student, living in the kind of luxury known only to the Shah of Iran. And all this for $38.50 a month.

Our landlord was none other than Caltrans, the state highway authority. Caltrans had condemned this property, and scores like it along the ridge, under the principle of eminent domain. Any minute now they would be razing the structures and constructing the new freeway. That "minute," however, was not to arrive for quite some years. State law required Caltrans to rent the facilities until they were physically eliminated. The uncertainty of not knowing month to month when we might be evicted was assuaged by strolling the grounds, lolling poolside, and perpetually partying.

I sat at my station before the sophisticated, then-state-of-the-art film editing machine, the KEM flatbed courtesy of the unknowing Regents of the University of California via C&B Feco. Diligently I cut and re-cut and re-re-cut *Extra Hot Sauce*. After I had viewed the jumble of disconnected footage repeatedly, my judgment became at last so clouded that I was able to consider the possibility that I had something resembling a rough cut.

Out of either inspiration or desperation—or great big gobs of both—one night I summoned my roommates poolside. Slade protested. He was in the midst of studying his Hebrew tapes.

"You're learning Hebrew?"

"Why not? Jews have been prominent in the civil rights movement since its inception, and for this I truly admire their courage, their conviction, their commitment to moral idealism and ethical principle. Additionally," he added, "they have a stranglehold on the movie business."

"I beg your pardon?"

"If you're a Jew, you got it made in Hollywood," Slade explained.

"But I know a catalog of Jews who are croaking," I told him. I listed seven or eight recent graduates of the film school whom I'd come to know at least superficially—Rabinowitz, Greenblatt, Schwartz, Lebowitz, Schine, and Steinhauer—who were unable even to get arrested in Hollywood.

"Nope," Slade Sloan insisted. "As surely as water flows downhill, Jews control the movie business. Don't misunderstand me," he went on. "You don't have to be a Jew. You have merely to learn their language."

"Their language?"

"Absolutely. Jews have their own country. Israel. You never heard of the Six Day War? It was in all the papers. Whatever language they speak in their own country has to be the language of the Jews, right? It's called Hebrew. Here, wait a second, listen to this." He peered down at the text that accompanied his set of reel-to-reel tapes. And then proudly he announced: "Shalom!"

I managed one way or another to extricate Slade from his studies and along with our other roomies got him out to the pool, where I aimed a projector through the sliding glass doors. We slouched on vinyl-webbed aluminum chaise lounges and guzzled Red Mountain wine directly from the jug—$1.39 a gallon at Lucky Mart—and puffed grass-laced tobacco as we watched images of *Extra Hot Sauce* play out upon the white, pocked-and-pebbled stucco wall of the pool equipment shed.

When the final, flickering frame faded, blond beach boy Troy pronounced the film "Trippy!"

"Far out!" pale, polite, neat-as-a-pin Perry agreed.

Maybe there was merit to this film after all, I allowed myself to wonder.

"Bullshit," Veronica said, dashing my hopes. "Stuart has been right all along. This film stinks. It commits the single most grievous sin art can commit. It's boring."

"Even tits and ass and dick get tedious by the three thousandth frame," Slade Sloan agreed. He shook his head in despair. "They'll flunk us out of film school."

"Worse," Veronica said, "they'll keep us there."

My mind raced. Was there no way in the world to salvage this wretched excess of naive, masturbatory, amateur, adolescent film-student excess? "Maybe there's a way to avant-garde it through," I said quietly, more to myself than to anyone else.

"By showing it upside down and backwards?" Veronica joked.

"That's part of it," I agreed.

"By distributing wine and dope to the audience?" Perry inquired.

"We've got ample wine and dope right here and the film still looks like piss," Veronica said.

I turned to Troy. "Crank up the tube," I commanded.

"What?" he said.

"Turn on the television."

"You want me to turn on the television?" he asked me.

"What gives you that idea?" I said. "You think that, because I asked you twice to turn on the TV, I want you to turn on the TV?"

Veronica looked at me with the narrowing gaze I had come both to welcome and to fear. Without turning toward Perry, she instructed him, "Do it."

Perry switched on the portable TV that sat on the patio. It slowly came aglow with Rowan and Martin in conversation with Merv Griffin. "Well!" Merv said. "Dick! Dan!" And he stared at them in broadly smiling silence. Here was a guy whose considerable fortune resided entirely upon his ability to gush without making a sound.

"Give me the Arri," I said.

"Do it," Veronica ordered Troy.

While Troy went to fetch the camera, I seized the channel knob and scanned the stations. Here was Johnny doing his monologue—it had to do with how crazy, how wild and weird and wacky everybody was out there in California. Here was Ralph Williams hawking fine-quality otto-mobiles and volume—he pronounced it "vah-yum"—merchandizing. Here were Dick Cavett and the Maharishi Mahesh Yogi. Here was the *George Putnam Channel Five News* with Vietnam war footage. Here was *The Big News* on KNX with snow-white-haired old-before-his-time from-the-desert-to-the-sea-to-all-of-Southern-California Jerry Dunphy and Vietnam war footage. Here was KNBC news with local anchor Tom Brokaw and Vietnam war footage.

Brokaw's on-air partner was a woman named Kelly Lang. Because Brokaw had such terrible difficulty pronouncing the letter "l," I was convinced Lang's hiring was an attempt by some executive to force Brokaw from his job.

And here was KABC-TV news with the co-anchor Judd brothers and Vietnam war footage.

And here was, at last, Troy returning with the Arriflex.

I seized the camera from him, hoisted it to my shoulder, trained the lens on the video screen, and hit the button. Not releasing the switch, not removing my eye from the reflex viewer, I called out, "Change it!"

Troy switched channels.

"Again!" I barked after perhaps ten seconds.

Troy changed channels once more.

"Ditto!" I said after a moment.

Troy obediently flipped the selector.

"And again!" I said, and again Troy performed as told.

After some minutes of filming various channels directly from the flickering, strobing tube, I ordered him to shut it off and get into the pool.

"The pool?" He turned off the television set and looked at me curiously.

"Now!" I insisted.

"Naked?"

"No," I told him, and he seemed just slightly disappointed.

I shut off the camera and turned to Slade. "Go!" I said.

"Where?"

"Pool!"

My vision fell now upon a poolside barbecue grill that was wrapped in a clear plastic dry-cleaning sack. I regarded it with satisfaction.

"Stuart?" Veronica said.

I cut her off. "Pool!"

"Me?"

"Do it!"

I carefully removed the transparent plastic covering from the grill and wrapped it completely around the still-grinding Arriflex. I seized a short end of broad, steel-gray gaffing tape and sealed the seams, rendering the sack watertight. To the consternation of the others, I tossed the entire contraption into the pool. Without another thought, fully clothed I followed the camera into the water, dove down, and retrieved it from the bottom.

I surfaced to find Slade, Troy, Perry, and Veronica staring down at me from the side of the pool, looking at me as if I'd gone bonkers. "What are you waiting for?" I asked them.

Collectively they shrugged, and now, wearing all their clothes, they leaped into the pool.

10

RELATIVE TO OTHER FORMS of expression—music, painting, sculpture, literature, poetry, drama, dance—film is in its infancy. Perhaps that's why there is among film folk an unholy obsession with finding and creating tradition even where it barely exists.

The USC film school is an example. At a university, at any institution, everything and everybody has to have a number. The number of the ragged but comfy main screening room at the cinema department was 108. Years later, when George Lucas built his alma mater a new facility, he insisted that the screening room—even though located on an upper floor in another building far removed from its original site—continue to be designated 108.

The projectors in old 108's bunkerlike cinder-block booth were standard professional carbon-arc machines intended for full-sized theaters. Here, however, the throw from lens to screen was so stunted that images were wonderfully, preposterously bright. In 108 the worst movie in the world—with the possible exception of *Last Year at Marienbad*—was worth viewing merely for its silver-screen sizzle. This was, after all, the sixties, and depending upon what had been smoked, popped, or dropped, one could occupy hours sitting close to the screen merely watching the grain dazzle, churn, roil, and seethe like so many turbulent marbles.

On-screen right now in 108 were curious, quirky, cascading images of every description. Here was Slade and here was Veronica, both fully clothed underwater, swirling around and around each other, their hair standing straight up, now rippling this way, that way. And here were images of the two now naked, now on the hard, black asphalt floor of the soundstage, sweating, rolling around one another, upside down, head to head, groin to groin, head to groin, groin to head, connecting, coupling, combining, colliding, conjoining.

This was all now abruptly replaced for exactly one second with the grainy black-and-white appearance of Johnny Carson, inch-wide television scan lines—subtle electronic stripes—running across his smiling Nebraska face. After Johnny it was Merv Griffin, then Perry, then Troy, then Merv again saying, "Dick! Dan!," then soldiers medevac'ed from Vietnamese terrain, then Veronica naked, Veronica clothed, Slade clothed, Slade naked, the two wet, the two dry, one dry and the other wet, the other wet and the one dry, Ralph Williams and his front line of specials, then Dick Cavett, then the Maharishi inquiring, "Bud whad is dee point of any-ding? Yes? No? Yes?," laughing his serene, knowing, mirthful, merry giggle.

These basic images, plus no small sampling of assorted odd, eccentric, disconnected graphics, were mixed and matched, shuffled and juggled, until at long last the tail title credit, *Extra Hot Sauce,* crawled across the screen and the house lights came up.

The roomful of students, faculty, and assorted hangers-on erupted in a firestorm of thundering, stamping, stomping, roaring approval that sustained itself for some several minutes and felt like a good half-hour. When finally it died down, Chairman Kevin Burns rose and faced a row of gray-bearded souls seated in the first row of risers behind the sound mixing panel. "Gentlemen?" Burns said.

Veronica, Slade, Perry, Troy, and I all sat in nervous anticipation awaiting the jury's verdict.

Pete Jenner, the camera instructor, who appeared at this moment uncharacteristically sober—and here it was practically noon already—took a deep breath and said, "A waveform monitor and shutter angle adjustment would have eliminated the video strobe."

Mike Kensei, the compact, puffy little Buddha of a sound professor, said, "A low-distortion signal generator, the Tektronix SG505, for example, could clean the hiss from your room tone track."

The head of the production program, a tranquil old fellow named John Davilla, said quietly, "I kinda like that movie." Davilla was able always to remain wholly, perfectly calm even in the midst of the worst bureaucratic turmoil. One day while I was standing over him in his office, awaiting his signature in triplicate on some long-forgotten waiver, he pulled open his top desk drawer and I discovered the source of his tranquillity: pills.

The editing instructor, a diminutive, introspective soul eating an egg salad sandwich from a brown bag, the eggs and mayonnaise smearing his chin as he spoke, said, "Compositionally, you refuse to relinquish frame. Cinematic image is more than reproduction. It's an entity of nature. A mold. A masque."

The directing instructor, Colin Douglas, a ruddy, cynical Brit who had burned out without ever having caught fire in the first place, said, "I didn't like that movie."

The film history–criticism guy, Carter Elliott, with thick linen-white hair swept back in a fussed-over Cesar Romero wave that was so full you could have surfed it, offered, "A splendid effort." He nodded with satisfaction, but now his eyes narrowed. He was notorious for asking this same question of every student project: "But does it work as a film?"

"How should it work?" Chairman Burns asked, arching his eyebrows. "As a shoehorn? A can opener? A pair of socks?"

The writing teacher, fat, flatulent, dyspeptic, dying Gordon Michaels, popping a small white pill under his tongue, growled, "I wrote a picture similar to this—under a nom de plume, of course—some years ago during the blacklist days."

"I don't doubt it," said moderator Kevin Burns disparagingly. The chairman took a moment to fire up an all-too-appropriate pipe. "This picture is a hodgepodge of stuck-together images signifying nothing," he said at last. "It's empty, hollow, pretentious in the extreme, silly, self-conscious, self-important, masturbatory." He sucked noisily on the pipe, his spit popping and crackling like distant small-arms fire. "In other words," he continued, "it's a perfect candidate for the student film festival circuit. The Europeans will eat it up—they'll say it's so *américain*. I can hear it now." Affecting a fair approximation of a French accent, he said, "The lovers clothed, unclothed, underwater, overwater, struggling to combine with each other against a tide of merchandising, death, comedy, tragedy."

Myself, all this time I could think only of Veronica. I was splendidly aware of the way she looked at me out of the corner of her eye, as if she were seeing me for the first time. Was it newfound respect with which she regarded me? Could she believe my crazy, stupid scheme had actually saved her little movie?

11

WAS this SUCCESS?

Student filmmaking, up to now an academic backwater, was enjoying expanded attention. Reporters began tramping through SC's
cinema department, shooting, interviewing. *Time* magazine ran an
article containing a photograph of my very own self, posed, inspecting a length of film alleged to be part of *Extra Hot Sauce*; never
mind that the footage I held in the photo was thirty-five-millimeter
and *Extra Hot Sauce* was shot in sixteen.

Interestingly, I was coming to feel that Veronica Baldwin, fire of
my loins, was awarding me serious attention. And it wasn't merely
because at last we'd been to bed; who had not shared Veronica's
bed? The deal was done late one night on the carpet alongside the
KEM flatbed where we'd been cutting; she decided suddenly to take
me and I let her have her way. It was sweet beyond description and
at the same time also strangely unfulfilling. She had inititated the
physical exchange and I had loved her with every cell, spent myself
completely, yet even as she lay there beside me she seemed light-
years distant. Was she there and not there, both at the same time,
perhaps just a little bit like my mother?

Had my life become the weary Freudian cliché by which, in a

doomed attempt to relive some primitive childhood fantasy, a fellow falls for a girl just like the girl who married dear old Dad? But don't clichés get to be clichés because they are so dreadfully, horribly true?

The overall vector my emotions took was wretched, palpable depression. Confusion. I asked myself all the lame, old questions: Who am I? What do I want? Where am I going? Do the Dodgers have even a remote chance of finishing in the upper division this season?

Most especially I wondered what, if any, was my future with Veronica. I had become so obsessed with the woman that from moment to moment I contemplated (1) moving out of the house and never again having anything whatever to do with her and (2) pleading with her to marry me.

But before I could embrace either alternative, Veronica executed a preemptive strike. We happened to be at the Moviola, monkeying around with some last-minute trims and adjustments, when she yawned and said it was time to call it a night.

"There are just three questions remaining to be addressed," she told me. "First, should the step-printing in the opening sequence be two frames or three?"

"Four," I told her. "I ran tests. It gives us the ethereal, jerky, otherworld effect film competition judges love."

"Second," Veronica continued, "should the credits come at the head or the tail?"

"Myself," I responded, "I prefer head credits. Get them out of the way."

"Finally," she said, stretching luxuriously, seductively, yawning so widely you could have stuck an entire grapefruit in her mouth, "would you, Stuart Thomas, ever consider taking me, Veronica Baldwin, to be your lawfully wedded wife?"

I ignored the question not because it was clearly a joke but because it was not. I appreciated that Veronica was totally serious. But why in the world would a woman as driven as Veronica bother with a geek like me? Did she see me as potentially the perfect househusband? As a convenient, tolerable father to the child she would soon enough bear? As a beta yang to her alpha yin?

I was just about as confused as a fellow could be. For support, instead of returning to the campus shrink, I checked out a newly created storefront therapeutic psychology program that had been recommended in the *Los Angeles Free Press* when it was an actual newspaper and not a catalog of ads for "massage" parlors. The *Free Press* therapy critic had awarded this particular regimen three and a half couches.

The Breakdown Center promised "Liberation for the New Aquarian Age." Their "offices" were the deserted showroom of a defunct Buick dealer on La Brea above Wilshire, with soaped-over plate-glass windows.

I entered without an appointment, plunked down too, too much money—all I had on me, some forty bucks and change—and soon found myself seated naked on a cold, uncomfortable steel folding chair, surrounded by not one or two but four—count 'em—purported therapists. I had graduated from group therapy to a group of therapists. As near as I could tell, one was a man, one was a woman, one was neither, one was both. If you thought about it (definitely a mistake), the fee came to only about ten bucks per therapist, in itself not such a bad deal, especially in Richard Nixon dollars.

What did I get for my forty bucks? Stripped, whipped, surrounded, pounded, kneaded, mistreated, squeezed, teased, pinched, lynched, derided, French-fried, accused, abused, assaulted, battered, salted, buttered, torched, tortured, trashed, thrashed, bashed, brutalized, and belittled.

"Relax! You're tense!"

"You're stressed!"

One of them squeezed the skin over my shoulder until the pain was excruciating. "Don't you feel how uptight you are? I can feel the knot of uptightness right here!"

"And here!" said a compatriot, pinching my back.

"And here!" shouted another, who did not even touch me.

"Of course I'm tense," I defended myself. "Of course I'm stressed and uptight. You're hurting me. You're killing me."

"It's you who's hurting you."

"It's you who's killing you."

"You've got to get in touch with your feelings."

"You've got to stop avoiding your feelings."

"You've got to own and embrace your feelings."

"I am in touch with my feelings," I insisted. "I own and embrace my feelings. What I feel is terrible. What I feel is pain."

"Good!" a member of the team rejoiced.

"Let it out!" said another. "Let all the pain out!"

"How else will you ever feel better?"

"I'll feel better," I responded, "if you take your hands off me for a minute, if you quit torturing me."

"You're torturing yourself, don't you see? Here! Feel that knot? Do you feel it right here? That's the marriage you're considering! Why? Why in the world would you marry?"

"You tell me," I said.

"You tell you!" they responded in virtual unison. Then one of them took a solo. "Why not act responsibly and intelligently? Why not live together before marrying to see if you get along together?"

"We already live together," I said. "We don't get along at all. So I figure we might as well marry."

Collectively they seized the chair and all at once yanked it from beneath me. Like a Saturday-morning TV cartoon character, I remained suspended in the air for a beat, then came crashing to the floor.

"Chew!" one of their numbers ordered me. "Chew the carpet!" But there wasn't any carpet, only a scratched linoleum floor. "Let it out! Let the pain out!"

"Vomit!" instructed another. "Try to vomit!"

"Puke!"

"There's another reason," I mumbled. "I love her." I hesitated and then I added, "And there's yet another reason: She's pregnant." I paused and said, finally, "Perhaps even by me."

"I'm sorry," one of the therapists said, "but that's all the time we have for today."

12

WhO WAS it WhO occupied my body and utilized my name at that treacly, trendy, redwoodsy double wedding now so many years ago?

From down the mountain—if you could see through the smog—the vista was scrubby and brown. Thousands of feet above the valley, however, were lush, deep green forests of tall pine, and crystal-clear cool, dry air. Diamond-studded Lake Arrowhead sparkled beneath our assembled group like an acid hallucination, and anyone could have believed we were in the remotest corner of the high Sierra instead of fifty-five minutes from downtown Los Angeles.

A ribbon-laced canopy of branches and leaves covered the principals and preacher; the sixty or seventy witnesses arranged themselves in a semicircle just slightly downslope from the ceremony. Nine men and women strummed guitars, for the most part quite poorly; worse, five well-intentioned folks blew flutes. And naturally, as if by state decree, uncounted numbers rattled tambourines. Even on drugs it sounded dreadful, the dopeheads reported later. A handful among them were still toking on joints, but there were also increasing numbers of souls covertly snorting white powder, sniffling, sneezing, and snorting yet again.

My own parents and Veronica's graced us with their presence. Veronica's mom, as we had advised, wore casual California street wear and comfortable shoes. Predictably, however, my mother wore a formal dress with a formal label, and flawlessly negotiated the uneven terrain in spiky patent heels. She sauntered in and rearranged all the arrangements, issuing orders to clergy and celebrants alike. As always, the easiest way to handle Mom—not just for me but for everybody—was to do precisely as instructed.

The fathers wore suits, but had the presence of mind to sling the jackets over their shoulders, very much in the manner of the guy in the Camel Filters ads. Veronica's dad removed his tie completely, rolled it up, and stuck it in his pocket; my own merely loosened his knot. In fairness, let us note that for him such an act was tantamount to flat-out, buck-naked anarchy.

Everybody else wore paisley, sandals, thongs, saris, shorts, tie-dyed tank tops and tees, bell-bottom jeans, jeans, jeans, and jeans.

There were headbands in abundance.

Both sets of parents were on their best behavior, acting as if they actually liked one another. And they were generously tolerant of what was to them clearly repugnant, this trashing of tradition. Happily, if they managed somehow to pretend to respect one another, they managed also to pretend to respect even us, their children. I was grateful that at least for the day there were no parental scenes, no tantrums, no power plays. But I was discomfited by the somewhat unholy attention my mom seemed to visit upon Veronica's dad, following him around, cutting him out of the herd like a cowboy on a roundup, whispering to him privately, urgently.

"Dearly beloved," began the overfed, underloved mail-order cleric, his purple satin robe—cut from a remnant, cinched with a clothesline—rippling in the breeze. All four parents winced as he read from scraps of crumpled ruled yellow legal paper, "We are gathered in this vortex, this ever-resonating orb . . ." Wasn't it merely one more all-too-perfect peace-and-love let-it-all-hang-out flipped-out freaked-out hipped hyped extravaganza celebrating the sweetness and stupidity that were the sorely overappreciated sixties?

It was crazy enough that Veronica, now visibly pregnant, and I pledged our lives to each other. Still wilder was the union of Slade, Perry, and Troy. Back then, gays were still pretty much fags, and it was a big deal even merely to admit to one's homosexuality, much less boast about it. An even bigger deal was a ménage—never mind its gender—seeking the blessing of the state.

"I now pronounce you," the preacher said to the trio, "man, man, and man, man."

Soon enough a banquet was under way. Instead of the usual un-healthful fare—beef, wheat, sweets—a wholly macrobiotic table was laid, featuring brown rice cooked in sesame broth, sliced and diced organic radishes, and as a beverage, instead of alcoholic poisons like wine and beer, lukewarm, pale green sun tea.

Truth to tell, we all would have starved if somebody hadn't made a mercy run into town for a few hundred dollars' worth of Big Macs and sixteen cases of politically incorrect Coors.

13

WhAt bEtteR WAY tO celebrate our honeymoon?

Klieg lights raked the foggy night. The banner festooning the entrance to the old Academy Theater proclaimed: "2nd Annual International Student Film Festival." Only a year earlier, seats had gone begging; indeed, questions were raised regarding the wisdom of holding another such event. The crowds now swarming the sidewalk offered ample testimony to the newfound and burgeoning interest in the world of student film.

Mobs of disappointed patrons, turned away for lack of seating, spilled out onto Melrose, Santa Monica, and Doheny. Surrendering any and all chance of gaining entry, many fled to the Troubadour bar; others got on line at Café Figaro. Still others prowled the aisles of Carl's; when all other forms of entertainment fail, Angelenos retreat to their twenty-four-hour supermarkets.

Clearly, the academic movie community was gaining not only public attention but Hollywood's, too, as among the fortunate few admitted to the screening were major players from the major agencies and the major studios. Here was UA's David Picker; there was CMA's David Begelman. And those were just the Davids. Here were

Warner's Ted Ashley and John Calley; there was Paramount's Charlie Bluhdorn; there was Fox's Gordon Stulberg.

Inside, the two bronze-colored oversized vinyl Oscars standing left and right of the screen glowed in the ambient light of the tail credits from *Extra Hot Sauce*. When at last the final card crawled to the top of the frame and vanished into the drapes, and the house lights came up, the pin-drop silence was smashed by a rumbling, thundering ovation. My first impression was that it was an aftershock of the Sylmar quake, and I feared Veronica, at my side, would go into labor then and there.

At last, upon the coaxing of our film school cronies—seated in front of us, behind us, on either side of us—we rose and stood awkwardly along with Slade, Perry, Troy, and a handful of others among our crew, cringing, gawking, wincing in the torrent of approval pouring down upon us.

Notwithstanding our aw-shucks posture, our what's-the-big-deal furrowed brows, the adoration of some several thousand tuxedoed souls was pleasurable in the extreme. It was obvious we had all died and gone to heaven. And what was heaven if not the original Academy of Motion Pictures Arts and Sciences Theater?

Now an ancient man with a crooked spine, clutching an aluminum walking stick, supported also by a young attendant, slowly made his painful way to center stage. Here was no less an eminence than Marcel Baudrillard himself, the French master film theoretician. Upon his introduction he, too, basked in the glory of his own ovation, and it was some little while before he could proffer his reaction to our humble movie.

"And zare, lay-deeze and gentlemans," he said in a voice that was stronger than one would have expected from so frail a presence, in an accent so thick you could stir it with an oar, "you are to having our gran' prize ween-aire. C'est marvelous, non? Zo *américain!* Ze lovers clozed, unclozed, under ze water, over ze water, struggling to combine wiz each other against ze tide of merchandising, death, comedy, and—how do you to zaying him?—*la tragédie.*"

After a thoughtful pause he said, "Shall we to honoring ze young film artistes?" Wielding the walking stick like an elaborate pointer, he gestured broadly to the crowd and the cheers and applause began again. And again we found ourselves half-reluctantly, half-eagerly rising, marinating in the trillion-decibel acclamation.

14

STARVING STUDENTS ONE DAY, celebrities the next:
Is that not Hollywood's organizing principle? Through all the newfound attention and activity and adulation and anticipation, the
phone calls, the telegrams, the invitations, solicitations, vibrations,
and excitations, one fact alone remained unchanged: We continued
to starve.

Our film festival triumph launched for us the movie business
course and curse: meetings. We enjoyed drive-on passes to the studios, even though—thanks to our undependable clunkers—we often traveled by bus. We enjoyed frequent and wildly enthusiastic
meetings in which we pitched ideas to eagerly nodding heads. Anything and everything we said—even "Hello, how are you?"—was
applauded, sometimes even before we said it. These upbeat, re-
soundingly affirmative conferences were followed inevitably by gaping, yawning, empty, hollow silence.

The faces we met belonged to producers; what we did not understand was that in Hollywood a producer was anybody with a
dime and access to a phone booth.

One guy said he had his whole movie worked out; it required
merely to be written and produced. To enlighten us, he slapped a

record on the stereo, a contemporary minor hit (I do not refer to the key), "Kaiser Bill's Batman," a curious, heavy-handed polka-ish Austrian instrumental. Mystified as we were, we tapped our fingers and swayed up and back as if we understood. He volunteered that drugs were now hot and there ought to be a lot of funny drug scenes. He had researched the narcotics subculture and suggested, for example, that in the movie we could have one character accidentally sit down on another's LSD needle.

Meetings with legitimate producers—we came to wonder if the phrase wasn't oxymoronic—proved every bit as futile as those with pretenders; indeed, it was impossible to tell the two apart. At the old Columbia Studios at Gower and Sunset, for example, we sat in overstuffed chairs facing overstuffed executives who grew downright moist as we lobbed notions at them.

They promised to get back to us.

We attended one meeting that was held in a limousine. Veronica sat on the jump seat, her legs dangling through the open door; her pregnancy was now so advanced she could fit no further into the vehicle. The Middle Eastern producer told us he loved our movie and would support us in any venture—regardless of subject matter— as long as it cost less than two million dollars. The meeting was interrupted, however, by two men with a court order and a tow truck; mid-pitch they repossessed the limo.

At Chasen's, with Veronica now gigantic as a whale and snorting smoked sardines and chocolate milk, a producer in a beige leisure suit told us that he loved our movie and would support us in any venture—regardless of subject matter—as long as it cost over two million dollars. Damned if he hadn't forgotten his wallet, however, and we ended up fronting the lunch tab. The chocolate milk alone was $4.25, and that was in Gerald Ford dollars.

In a modest little beach cottage in the colony at Malibu—it was then worth nearly $50,000—a potbellied, pot-smoking producer in bikini swim trunks, the tip of his pecker peeking plain as day over the frayed elastic band, told us that he absolutely loved our movie and would support any venture regardless of subject matter, regardless of cost, as long as it was set in a location where he had frozen funds: Lapland.

What else could funds be in Lapland, we wondered, except frozen?

A few years later, the humble seaside cottage would turn over for something north of $4 million, and two months after that would be swept to sea in the El Niño–powered storms of '81–'82.

The young men among us remained eligible for the draft, so we continued to hang around the university, enrolling each semester for two credits of Directed Independent Study. One afternoon, Troy, browsing in the student store, shoplifted a copy of Abbie Hoffman's *Steal This Book*. He got exactly as far as the exit before security guards seized him.

Troy's case never got to any court of law; he negotiated a settlement whereby he dropped out of school and promised never again to darken Tommy Trojan's door. But now he was, of course, in need of another student draft deferment scam, and for expedience alone he enrolled in a Texture-coated fly-by-night institution on South Vermont: Lenny and Larry's Law School. His major: whiplash. His minor: tax shelters. All that was required for admission was the ability to sign the tuition check. He borrowed some of the money from his folks and turned tricks in West Hollywood to earn the rest. "It's a whole lot less degrading than waitressing," Veronica volunteered, when Perry and Slade expressed jealous outrage over Troy's johns.

Astonishingly, Troy found himself actually attending classes at the law school as he had but rarely at USC film school. We picked him up in the van one day only to receive a crazed, manic lecture regarding nonrecourse notes and accelerated depreciation. "It leverages the principal sixfold," he explained to us with a straight face. "We have merely to four-wall the product in two markets to shelter convertible bonds and have them treated as capital gains. Even if the venture loses money, therefore, it makes money. Understand?"

We all sat with blank expressions.

"Product?" I heard myself asking Troy, as I scanned backward through his bizarre speech. "Venture?"

"Movie," he explained, his patience straining. "Nobody with brains in his head is going to invest in a movie. We'll raise the money ourselves."

"But even if we found funds for a movie," Veronica asked, "what would we shoot?"

"That," Troy answered, "is up to Stuart."

"It is?" Veronica and I asked in unison.

"You're our writer," Troy explained.

"I am?"

"Aren't you?" Veronica asked me. "You still owe Professor Gordon Michaels a script for his advanced screenwriting course, right?"

"But I haven't the foggiest—"

"Something esoteric and personal," Perry said, warming to the notion. "Make it a delicate film, Stuart. A quiet film. Something that causes to resonate in the viewer a reflection of his own humanity."

"Fuck, no," Veronica snapped. "We already did our artsy-craftsy number. We need something commercial. We need a hit."

"An exploitation picture?" I asked.

"Exactly." Veronica nodded.

"Sure," Slade affirmed. "Then, after this film, we can film the kind of film we want to film."

We slid up the ramp onto the 10 at Hoover, came around left onto the 11, segued into the 5 and headed north to the 2 until we reached our rancho-palazzo on Roundtop Drive.

Parked at rude angles in front of the house—as if they had arrived in a hurry—were several LAPD black-and-whites.

15

the FRONT DOOR WAS wide open and uniformed officers paraded in and out in a steady stream. They carried much of our precious filmmaking equipment.

Indeed, at this very moment, as I helped the unwieldy Veronica from the van, we saw two officers struggling on either end of the KEM flatbed editing machine. They maneuvered it toward a stake truck that was just now arriving and set it on the power lift.

"Where do you think you're going with that?" Veronica challenged the officers.

"Who's asking?" the uniform inquired.

Veronica identified us all.

"Please step to the sidewalk," the officer said, and reluctantly we all obeyed. He brandished a legal-sized document, waved it in our faces. "This is a search warrant." He peered closely at the document. "We've seized one KEM flatbed editing machine, serial number A-1000941, two Nagra sound recorders, serials 476HB19 and 476GR63, also a self-blimped Arriflex sixteen-millimeter motion picture camera, a six-gang synch block, and some various other assorted items of equipment, all of them the property of the Regents of the University of California."

Another officer began handcuffing the lot of us as yet another informed us, "You are under arrest. You have the right to remain silent. In the event you choose to speak . . ."

Still fairly new to California, and already I was being read my *Miranda* rights for the second time.

Veronica was taken to Sybil Brand Institute for Women and the rest of us were scattered all over the city in various holding facilities. Soon enough, I found myself dressed in an orange jumpsuit at some gloomy Valley jail. As it happened to be the Friday of a holiday weekend, three full days would pass before I could get sprung.

The prison was grim but manageable. Notwithstanding a desperate poverty of resources, there was a bit of a library and even an abandoned, functioning antique Underwood portable. I bribed a guard with my watch and he provided me with a ream of paper. Three days' incarceration was exactly what I needed to pound out our exploitation screenplay, a bikers' tale that seemed to me every bit as crude as the place where it was written.

I was typing the final FADE OUT mid-afternoon on Tuesday when a guard tapped me on the shoulder to tell me I was free to leave the hotel. With the script tucked under my arm, I made my way to the entrance, and like a con in a Jimmy Cagney–Eddie Robinson picture, I squinted as I emerged into the Southern California sunshine.

Greeting me was Veronica, and in her arms a beautiful baby as black as ebony. And even though the child was puffy and wrinkled like the newborn she was, she already possessed sufficient personality and physical features to be recognized for what she also was: a Slade Sloan clone, only darker. Veronica had delivered the baby in the infirmary at Sybil Brand.

Slade Sloan aside, the baby was immediately our own, mine and Veronica's only. I handed Veronica the screenplay and she passed me our child. Trembling, I held her sweet, precious little body in my arms and regarded her with wonder and with awe, counting limbs and digits again and again and again.

And from that very moment I loved my little daughter completely, wholly, without reservation; I experienced emotions I never before knew to exist. My till-then narrow, limited life was instantaneously and irrevocably expanded beyond all horizons. I knew that I had been liberated from the petty and mundane, that I was as happy as it is possible to be. I clucked and cooed and cuddled and rejoiced with no thought whatsoever of doing anything else again.

We named the baby Raynebeaux.

We named the screenplay *Brutal Bad-ass Angels.*

16

THE LOVERS—HERE MERE dots on the sprawling land-
scape—appeared to prance merrily across a gently sloping field
awash with wildflowers of every hue. The young man and woman
linked their fingertips in blissful union. From this vast distance there
was no sound save the hot, rising wind, but it was easy to imagine
Mozart or Vivaldi in the background and here and there a breathy
feminine giggle and a throaty male chortle.

Closer, however, the scene was altogether different. For one thing,
from the expressions on the couple's faces, it was clear the mood
was not joy but fear, not romantic abandon but panic and dread.
Sweat streaked their foreheads and dampened their temples. They
gulped air and wheezed in agony, their weary legs sprinting for what
looked to be their lives.

Then, in the distance, came the sound. No lush, serene string
section, it was an ominous, numbing rumble, an otherworldly buzzing of bees, a growling of bears. As the sound rose in volume, it
became clear that there were neither bees nor bears but, instead,
dozens of two-stroke engines, humming, straining against the terrain.

There now popped into view upon the horizon a horde of motorcyles. They cut a swath through the tall, burnt-blond grass, the buttercups, the honeysuckle, wisteria, chokecherry, soapwort, arrowroot, acacia, star thistle, shepherd's purse, foxglove, and hepatica, closing upon the fleeing pair. Soon the bikers encircled the couple completely. The lovers came to a frantic, panting halt, now feinting this way, that way, all to no avail as the choppers rode around and around their exhausted prey.

Gritty, gristly leather-clad riders drooled and snarled, their voices sounding very much like their engines. Cutting off all avenues of escape, the Hell's Angels taunted the couple with curses and wicked, psychotic laughter.

"Leave her be," pleaded the young man. "Take me." Overcome by the crazed bravado born of desperation, he drew himself up to his full height and postured defiantly before his tormentors. "Take me," he said again, "if you're man enough."

Their answer was to abandon the bikes where they stood and to seize the young man, pummeling him mercilessly. Bones popped, snapped, and crackled like so much breakfast cereal; hair tore from flesh with a chilling white whisper reminiscent of Velcro unfastening.

As the young man lapsed toward unconsciousness, his oppressors surrounded him in an ever-tightening ring. They unzipped their flies, whipped out their members, and urinated beer-fueled steaming yellow streams upon him. At last, their bladders spent, their attention turned to his companion. "No!" she pleaded as the fat, filthy bikers advanced slowly, evenly toward her.

They grabbed her, tore at her clothes. In a flash she was quite naked, her porcelain-white skin fairly flashing in the bright sunshine, her golden tresses gleaming. There was dreadful quiet as the predators regarded their defenseless victim with perverse glee.

Now, suddenly, they scuffled among themselves for the chance to beat her head, shoulders, back, thighs, and breasts, all the while bellowing and belching. Throwing her bruised, scraped body upon the ground, they ripped their jeans to their knees. Three at a time they fell on her, one at one end, two at the other, raping her again and again and again and again. Her protests grew feeble, her eyes glazed over.

"Cut!" Veronica called from the edge of the set, behind the phalanx of camera, crew, and equipment. Wide-eyed from her mother's backpack, idly sucking on a shiny yellow plastic 35mm film core, baby Raynebeaux watched the action. "Cut!" Veronica insisted as the Angels hesitated another moment before backing away from the fallen actress.

The male lover now arose unscathed from the grass where he lay. A crew member handed him a roll of paper towels and he unspooled several sheets and mopped his piss-soaked face. Donning a bathrobe tossed her by a grip, the young woman also rose to her feet. "Can we try that once more?" she inquired earnestly. "I know I can give you a better reading."

"That's a wrap for today," Veronica informed everyone who was assembled, checking her watch. She turned to the actress and explained, "Too late, sweetie." She gestured toward the sky, where the still-bright afternoon sun was just beginning to encroach upon the horizon. "The color temperature is crashing," she explained.

Veronica, in fact, would not have shot the scene again under any circumstances. It had succeeded well enough and our producer, Troy, his finger perpetually on the ledger, never would have permitted the expenditure of extra raw stock, to say nothing of film production's single most costly commodity: time. "Trust me," Veronica reassured the actress, "you were beautiful."

"Atmosphere!" Troy shouted. The thoroughly pliant, docile bikers assembled in an orderly line. "Sign your vouchers," he commanded, distributing legal-sized forms among them, "if you expect to get paid." He added after a moment, "And if you don't know how to sign your name, just scrawl your mark." Mincing just a bit, he proffered a pose that was distinctly fey.

In a last attempt to demonstrate her devotion to art, the actress turned now to me. "But I can give a superior reading," she insisted. "Tell them to let us have just one more shot at it."

Before I could disappoint her, Troy said, "Honey, why are you asking him? He has no say in any of this."

I nodded at her sheepishly and offered by way of explanation, "I'm merely the writer."

17

TIMID, LIFELONG MIDDLE-CLASS KID, I had never before ridden a motorcycle. And now here I was atop no mere bike but a monster Harley 1965 Panhead, the last of its breed, with sixty-three cubic inches of displacement, enough power to leap the Grand Canyon not from rim to rim but lengthwise.

I gripped the handlebars and tilted my body this way and that, alternately twisting the accelerator and squeezing the brake as appropriate to the terrain. All the while the wind whipped through my hair as, to my left, the bloodred sun hissed and sizzled as the glorious Pacific swallowed it whole.

Veronica was mounted on the bike directly beside me, the instant classic Shovelhead with its revolutionary V-twin seventy-four-inch engine. She reached around behind herself and managed somehow to liberate our sweetly squalling Raynebeaux from her backpack.

"Here," she called, shouting in order to be heard above the din of wind and traffic. She passed the child to me as we sped down the highway. I let go of both grips and received our beloved baby in my arms. Taking my eyes completely off the road, I gazed leisurely into her suddenly serene dark eyes. She was instantaneously peaceful near her daddy's heart. I knew yet again that I owned the entire planet and some substantial number of the leading galaxies.

To engage in such otherwise benign activities while riding motorcycles at high speed on a major thoroughfare might appear to have been reckless in the extreme but, in fact, along with a dozen others, our bikes were affixed securely to the long, flat bed of an open truck, part of the movie crew caravan.

And at last, with the light now faded, we pulled up to a warehouse in Venice, several blocks from the beach. A sign fronting the structure read: "Hell's Angels Enterprises, Ltd., A Wholly Owned Subsidiary of General National Group." The bikers unloaded the hogs and wheeled them into their modern, spacious headquarters, designed by no less than Charles Eames.

Slade, Perry, Troy, Veronica, and I, plus, of course, Raynebeaux, were boarding Slade's van for the journey back to our Hollywood cutting room when Zonker, the crusty, hirsute, middle-aged Angels leader, approached. "You guys care to come in for a cognac or seltzer or whatever? Apple juice for the kid?" Weary from the day's shoot, and with a night's editing in front of us, we were eager to depart, but out of politeness we consented to squander just another several minutes. It was not lost on us that we required the Angels' cooperation for yet a few more days.

Inside, as bikes were wheeled to storage in the rear, we moved past a plush reception area into a comfortable lounge with sleek vinyl furniture where various Angels girlfriends—Mamas—laid a broad table with hors d'oeuvres: delicate canapés, buckwheat-groat-stuffed baby mushroom caps, finger sandwiches with cucumber, crisp celery sticks, and carrots that had been scrubbed, not scraped or peeled. "All of the vitamins and minerals," Zonker explained, selecting a carrot and taking a delicate bite, "are in the skin, see. Most people, they scrape that right off, and what do you got?"

When no answer was offered, he provided his own. "Yellow-orange starch is what you got. Empty calories. You lose the fresh, sweet flavor, plus the essential nutrients." He offered a carrot stick to Raynebeaux and at first I worried that it was not appropriate for a liquids-only infant. But soon enough it became clear she could gum it and suck it and not liberate any particles that might lodge in her windpipe.

All of us rested except Troy, who scanned his ledgers with concern. "I don't see this spread in the budget," he muttered under his breath, gesturing toward the food and drinks.

"Our treat," Zonker said. "Have a seat. Enjoy. Eat a carrot. Scrubbed. Not scraped. Not peeled."

Troy warily cracked a Diet Pepsi and nibbled a finger sandwich. All the while he remained standing.

"Have a seat," Zonker insisted gently once again. He handed Troy a coaster. "The cans leave rings on the mahogany," he explained.

"Can't," Troy said. He turned to Veronica. "We have to get back to town and synch yesterday's dailies." Now he returned his gaze to Zonker. "And you guys need your rest for tomorrow's stunts."

"Tomorrow?" Zonker said. "We're busy tomorrow."

"Bet your ass you're busy tomorrow," Troy said. "We grab some cutaways of the rape sequence and then shoot the opening to the eye-gouging."

"Tomorrow," Zonker said, "we collect Christmas toys for underprivileged tots."

"Christmas in July?"

"Plan ahead," Zonker said.

Maneuvering to avoid a confrontation, Troy peered at his clipboard and its call sheets. "Okay," he said, nodding. "We put off tomorrow till the next day, postpone the amputation and shoot the toilet stuff, the vomiting," Troy explained. "Then we catch up with you Angels the day after tomorrow."

"The day after tomorrow," Zonker said, "we serve tea and crumpets at the senior citizens' center over by Temple Beth O'hev Shalom."

"What's going on here?" Veronica said. "We have a deal."

"You want little children to go hungry?" Zonker gushed, gosh-all-golly and wide-eyed.

"I thought it's toys for the kids," I said. "They're going to eat the toys?"

"It is not stomachs alone that know hunger," Zonker explained, "but also souls. Kids require toys to sustain and nourish them. They require affirmation and approval. If they don't receive them, children's spirits become warped and distended exactly as their bone and tissue are misshapen for lack of protein."

"Protein?" I said.

"Quiet!" Veronica insisted, shooting me the reprimanding glance I'd come to know all too well; as always, it caused me to shrink like a scolded schoolboy. I wondered yet again whether in the marriage to Veronica I had not replicated the configuration of personalities prevailing in my parents' house when I was a kid. She turned to Zonker. "How much do you want?"

"How much do we want?" Zonker repeated. "Why, what in the world can you mean? You suggest we invoke worthy causes merely to exploit narrow financial advantage?" He shook his head slowly, sadly. "I'm hurt," he said quietly. "I'm truly, genuinely hurt." He touched the corner of one eye, as if to blot a tear.

"How much do you want?" Veronica said again.

"Fifteen points off the gross from dollar one," Zonker said, "plus a sixty-forty prorated split on foreign distribution, and an accelerated schedule of participation retroactive to commencement of principal photography. A rolling break on sequels and TV spin-offs. Right of first refusal on the novelization, paperbound and/or cloth. Plus one hundred percent of all ancillary considerations—coffee mugs, T-shirts, and so on, any and all products that exploit the Hell's Angels trademark, with full approval of all uses of the logo in print ads and electronic media."

We all stood there speechless as he reached over to a nearby desk and opened the top drawer, from which he removed a sheaf of legal papers. He thrust it at Troy. "Here," he said. "It's all spelled out in this revised codicil to our agreement."

Troy scanned the documents. "Impossible." He looked up at Zonker now imploringly. "This whole project's financed on our parents' squandered tuition, credit cards, a hocked camera, a borrowed cutting room and equipment, and, I'll admit it, a trick or two or three on the Strip."

"Hand jobs only," Perry said. "All right, an occasional blow job," he admitted. "It's less degrading than waitressing."

"You're thieves," Troy told Zonker. "Extortionists."

"No, they're not," I said.

"Whose side are you on?" Veronica asked me in shock.

"They're not thieves," I insisted. "They're fairies!" Now I turned apologetically to Troy, Perry, Slade. "Metaphorically," I explained. "Figuratively."

"Fairies?" Zonker said.

"Next to you," I said, "the Campfire Girls are Hitler Youth." I turned to Veronica. "Let's shoot 'em," I told her.

"Just because people disagree is hardly any cause for violence," Zonker said.

"I'm not talking guns," I said. I turned to Troy. "Bring on the Panaflex."

Troy, shrugging in apparent despair, retreated toward the door.

"Face facts," Zonker said. "You need us. What can you do? Trash the whole script?"

"It's already trash," I said. "It was trash as I wrote it."

"But it's good trash," Veronica said. I rejoiced that she defended me.

"Nowhere as good as true-to-life trash," I said. I gestured toward the table. "Baby mushrooms stuffed with kasha, can you believe it? Carrots and celery sticks. Hell's Angels? Got any whiskey? Beer? Grass, pills, 'shrooms, mescaline, needles, 'ludes, coke, downs, ups, speed, acid, dust? Hell, no. Diet soda! Apple fucking juice. Fruit fucking punch. Here's our script. Here's our movie."

At this very moment Troy reappeared, leading our cinematographer, who wielded a hand-held camera. There was a moment's awkward silence, and then enlightenment appeared to crash down upon my beloved Veronica. "Sure!" she said, and turned to the cameraman. "Roll!"

"Roll?" he said.

"Make sure you get a close-up of the radish roses."

The cameraman switched on the camera and began filming. "Pan slowly across those lace doilies," Veronica instructed him. "This'll be a documentary, an exposé tearing the lid off the so-called Hell's Angels. Do they terrorize towns? Do they desecrate synagogues? Shucks, no. They're too busy helping little old ladies cross the street. They're all caught up cooperating with the police in their Toys for Tots campaign. They're preoccupied stuffing little butter-basted mushrooms and assorted delicate munchies."

"Not scraped or peeled but merely scrubbed," Troy mocked.

"Hang on a second," Zonker said. "Wait just one little minute there."

"Hold lovingly on those coquilles St.-Jacques," Veronica ordered the cameraman, whose instrument purred and fluttered smoothly, reassuringly.

"Fuck the coasters," Zonker said, puffing up like a poisonous, spiny blowfish. "Fuck the fucking lace fucking doilies." He ripped the doilies from the table and then yanked the entire tablecloth, sending the whole spread—dishes and finger sandwiches and glasses and apple juice—cascading to the floor in a crash that resembled Japanese wind chimes digitized and remastered at ten trillion decibels.

Then came the all-out brawl, mushrooms and dips sailing, furniture shattering, fists flying. Those of us among the film crew managed somehow to remain on the sidelines while Hell's Angels wrestled each other to the floor, transforming their previously Saran Wrapped space into a sticky, slippery shambles.

All the while Veronica led our cameraman on a grand tour of the place, cranking, grinding, filming the destruction. Perry, in the meantime, had switched on the Nagra and adjusted the attenuators as the needles peaked and sank and peaked again in response to the clatter.

Raynebeaux dropped her carrot and wailed. I seized yet another shiny yellow plastic 35mm film core from my pocket and thrust it to her lips. She sucked upon it greedily, instantly and totally placated.

18

iF the DAY WAS uncharacteristically muggy, the plush, carpeted screening room at AFIL was so cool, so crisp and dry that we shivered constantly and dosed our throats with Smith Brothers cherry cough drops, two at a time. The lab's initials stood for Amalgamated Film Industry Lab. Working-stiff moviemakers, however, aware of the outfit's penchant for misplacing footage, called them All Film Is Lost.

Teeth chattering, we sat there with the color-correction expert, Al, who wore mint socks, lime pants, a kelly-green shirt, an olive drab sport coat, and a turquoise tie. We watched scene after scene of *Brutal Bad-ass Angels* unfold on the stop-and-go projector as Veronica, Troy, and our director of photography commented on lights and filters. They were attempting to match various takes from various rolls and reels, in order to render the movie—by nature a scattered, shattered enterprise composed of shards and shreds and fragments—appear singularly seamless and whole.

At long last we approached something like satisfaction. Troy inquired when we could pick up a composite release print. Al pressed a buzzer on his board, and in a moment a figure of authority entered the chamber.

That we had managed one way or another even to shoot the movie, let alone get it edited and into the can, was no less than a miracle. But it was a miracle that cost some money. And the money had been generated largely by devices already explained to Zonker and the Angels: everything from maxed-out credit cards to prostitution.

Among these devices was also a deferment from AFIL. The lab had fronted all our raw stock and processing and printing services, postponing payment until the film was complete. Now, however, in an attempt to insure compensation, they explained that our charming exercise would be held hostage—the negative locked safely in their vault—until they were paid.

The lab would release to us in the meantime some dirty-dupe clips, crudely printed copies of key scenes, because they appreciated that without this weapon in our arsenal we had no way to raise the completion capital necessary to settle our account.

And that is how we came to find ourselves not a week later in the darkened doctors' lounge at a hospital in Panorama City with eight surgeons in green scrubs viewing the destruction playing out on a portable screen. One of the doctors even wore his surgical mask.

On the flickering, diminutive screen, Hell's Angels brawled and struggled, clobbering each other, rolling around on the floor amidst a mess of sticky, slippery fluids and foodstuffs. Through the tiny, tiny speaker, the crashing and clattering sounded a whole lot like paper being crumpled very close to the microphone.

Perched nervously in the rear, Veronica, Slade, Troy, and I—Perry was conspicuously absent—watched the doctors watch the movie. On screen, the party scene finally concluded and dissolved into an image of Hell's Angels riding down the coast before a hallucinatory tangerine-lavender California sunset.

At last, the end title, *Brutal Bad-ass Angels,* crawled across the screen.

And now the lights came up and Troy shut off the projector. He made his way to the front of the group and distributed sleek, shiny folders among the physicians. These contained all sorts of complicated fact-and-finance graphs and spreadsheets, eight-by-ten glossy production stills depicting not only scenes from the film itself but also images of the crew creating the movie. There were prospective one-sheets, lobby cards, proposed distribution and exhibition schemes.

Additionally, there were enhanced minibiographies of the principal artists. Only I, the writer, had been excluded from this material, but that was "merely a printer's error," Troy had patiently explained to me. I believed him.

He stood now before the assembled doctors. "As our prospectus clearly illustrates, a minimal investment-share participation leverages fourfold with regard to Internal Revenue purposes—creating, in effect, a paper loss worth a sizable deduction in the subsequent fiscal year."

A member of the audience called out, "But what if the movie shows a profit?"

"Impossible," Troy assured them. "You've seen our film. Permit me to assert with confidence, here is a uniquely dreadful, rotten, quite perfectly hopeless little picture." He swelled with pride when he said this, nodded, and strutted just a bit before the group, posturing not a little like Mussolini on his balcony.

We had to admire Troy's pluck, even if it appeared that his scheme was fairly futile.

Just now, however, a doctor rose from his chair. He was the one who wore not only scrubs but also his surgical mask. "Forgive me if I break in here," he mumbled through gauze, "but I've got to get back to a kidney transplant. Look, I'm sorry," he went on, "but the most I can possibly invest is twenty-five thousand." To the astonishment of everyone in the room, he whipped out a checkbook and commenced to write.

"We certainly appreciate your expression of confidence," Troy said, stunned, "but our structure requires us to limit participation to single increments of five thousand dollars per individual investor."

Undeterred, the doctor finished writing his check, ripped it from its binder, thrust it at Troy. "Twenty-five grand," he insisted, "take it or leave it," and without another word he fled the room.

"But," Troy stammered, "that just about sells us out."

Now, suddenly, the other doctors were on their feet. "Wait!" one shouted. "What'd you waste our time for? I want a piece of this action, damn it!" And he, too, scrawled out a check and crammed it into Troy's vest pocket.

"And how about me?" said another.

"And me!" said yet another.

The lot of them were now scribbling checks and raining them down upon Troy like so much confetti, and soon enough the medical lounge was emptying. We made our own way out of the room and down to the parking lot to Slade's sometimes trusty van.

Behind the wheel, waiting patiently, dressed in surgical scrubs, his mask now loose around his neck, was Perry, the "surgeon."

"They went for it?" he asked.

Troy joyfully waved the fistful of checks in his face.

19

With OUR FUNDING REPLENISHED, we were able to liberate *Brutal Bad-ass Angels* from the lab. In search of what Troy called a negative pickup deal, we screened it for all the major studios and every half-baked penny-pinching independent outfit festering at Hollywood's edge. When, after some months, not a single company appeared even remotely interested in distributing the picture, to fulfill Internal Revenue's tax-shelter requirements we struck a release print and four-walled the film in two domestic locations. That is, we rented the theaters ourselves and paid the projectionists out of our own pockets.

In the first venue, Brownsville, Texas, we naively organized a modest premiere. It proved just a trifle pathetic, as our little company of cast and crew far outnumbered the paying audience.

In the other, Bozeman, Montana, there was a state university campus, so we dredged up a "cinema appreciation" class, presumably to supply adoring students before whom we could strut and pose and perform our impression of successful Hollywood professionals. Instead, we were denounced by neo-Marxist semiotic feminist Francophile filmic theoreticians who, during the showing, killed a chicken in the theater and sprayed the screen with its blood. This represented a metaphor, they asserted, for the menstrual blood of oppressed Third World women across the globe and was a plea, more particularly, for justice in Palestine.

Years of litigation would be required to arrive at an agreement with the theater as to whose responsibility it was to restore the soiled screen.

Notwithstanding the fact that we now had an actual film under our belt, we returned to Hollywood still more obscure than when we had left. Tax-leveraged funding for films was soon, quite properly, restricted by legislatures, and opportunities for filmmakers grew increasingly narrow.

The State Highway Commission finally got around to building Route 2, the Glendale Freeway, and during some twenty minutes of an overcast spring morning a lone bulldozer reduced our formerly splendid manse to rubble. Veronica and I found a charming turn-of-the-century bungalow on a hillside in Echo Park and moved in just as our second daughter, Pacifica, was born. Unlike her big sister, this child was even biologically my own, as was evident even by merely glancing at her from a mile away.

Slade, Perry, and Troy found an apartment in Silver Lake and worked odd jobs in the movie business. Slade became a self-described "pussy barber," working for a producer of sex films, then called nudie cuties. By today's standards these represented preposterously tame fare. Indeed, there was no escaping the irony that our own humble *Extra Hot Sauce* was infinitely more explicit. Slade's assignment was to remove all frames in which pubic hair was visible.

Amazingly enough, as the sexual revolution hit the mainstream, standards quickly reversed and Perry later ended up working for the same producer; his assignment was to restore the same pubic hair in the very same films from which Slade had previously excised them.

Moreover, this all occurred in the very same cutting room we had borrowed to edit *Brutal Bad-ass Angels*.

It wasn't long before Slade, Perry, and Troy, weary of sucking around Hollywood's fringes, finally split for then-swingin' London to try their luck in what appeared to be the born-again British film industry. The Beatles had charged it with fresh life in *A Hard Day's Night*, and now there was extraordinary excitement in anticipation of the release of a film that could only soar both artistically and commercially: Charlie Chaplin's *A Countess from Hong Kong*, starring no less than Marlon Brando and Sophia Loren.

As for myself, I became something of a househusband; I spent my days hip-deep in toys at our Echo Park digs, wiping urine and projectile vomit from the walls. Days, with a single hand I picked and pecked at my typewriter, speculating on screenplays. "Speculating" meant, of course, that nobody paid for them. With the other hand I cuddled and coddled and bottle-fed Pacifica. And with my mouth and chin, barking and gesturing, I scolded and shepherded Raynebeaux.

Veronica freelanced as a director, winning an occasional commercial but mainly shooting clips for Scopatone, precursor to the music video. Scopatone was a jukebox with pictures. Instead of merely playing a record, the device spat out images of the performance onto a pale, flickering rear screen. Once I schlepped the girls set-side to see Mommy shoot Frank Sinatra, but it turned out to be Frank Sinatra, Jr.

My age, combined with my low lottery number plus my status as a parent, provided me now with sufficient points to eliminate any need for a student draft deferment. Moreover, the troops were being withdrawn. Still, I maintained my status at film school, for no reason that I clearly understood. Perhaps it was to keep me from owning up to the fact that I was already something like an adult. Perhaps it was for the small remuneration I earned as a teaching assistant.

The teacher I assisted was the nuttiest professor of them all: Jerry Lewis.

Amazingly enough, Lewis received an appointment as an adjunct professor at USC, where he taught a course in directing. Even students who actually loathed him—George Lucas among them—enrolled in the class simply because they hoped Lewis could win them their Directors Guild card and a job. In truth, by this time Mr. Lewis could just barely get himself a job.

I came to know him rather well, and I was surprised to discover that in real life Jerry Lewis was not nearly as crazy as his screen persona suggested; he was crazier. At the first class, for example, he strode through his entourage of hangers-on stark naked except for a floppy, oversized diaper.

He moved up to the lectern and studied the crowd most leisurely. After a long, long while he said quietly, "Cig me."

A flunky promptly materialized from the retinue, thrust a Gauloises into the professor's slight pout, whipped out a butane lighter, flicked on its foot-long flame, and fired up the cigarette. Lewis took a long drag and then another, expelling the blue smoke from his nostrils in two distinct streams that somehow never merged.

Then he said, "Drink me."

And yet another flunky emerged from the woodwork. He snapped open the bright brass catch on the lid of an elaborate oxblood attaché case. Various tiers of shelves arose and arrayed themselves, sporting glasses, bottles, ice. The flunky prepared what used to be called a highball, now cocktail, and proffered it to Mr. Lewis, who took a small, gentle sip that ended, somehow, with a loud, vulgar slurp that could have been heard in San Bernardino.

Jerry Lewis set the drink on the podium, stared long and hard at the crowd, and finally said, "Pill me."

Yet another drone appeared, wielding a vial of capsules. He shook out two brightly striped pills and handed them to his boss, who downed them with the booze.

Jerry Lewis was at his absolute worst when he became terribly, wretchedly serious. " 'True fops help nature's work and go to school,' " he said at last, " 'to file and finish God's almighty fool.' " He glared silently at the group. "Who said that?" he asked.

"You did," a student responded, smiling brightly.

"Schmuck!" Lewis snapped, annoyed. "Putz! I'm the comic here. I'm the goddamned movie star. You want to go joke-for-joke with me? Might as well go one-on-one with Lew Alcindor. Or vaccine-for-vaccine with Dr. Jonas Salk, who, by the way, just happens to be a dear, personal friend of mine."

A student rose from the ranked chairs. "John Dryden."

"Yes, John?" Jerry Lewis said.

"No, sir," the student said. "I mean John Dryden, English poet laureate and dramatist. He spoke the 'true fops—God's almighty fool' line." After a moment's hesitation, the student added, "In 1798, two years before his death."

"Who asked you?" Jerry Lewis said. "And how do you know he spoke the line? Did you hear him? Well? Did you? Did you?"

The student cringed in silence.

"All we surely know," Lewis continued, "is that he wrote the line. Am I right? Am I?"

Nobody in the class said a word.

"Who spoke the line?" Lewis said. When no one responded he said, "I did." And he laughed and chuckled and howled and salivated, his shoulders shaking, his diaphragm's movement plainly visible beneath his shirt. The laughter rolled and gurgled and appeared unstoppable. Now tears were streaming down his face. He turned to his entourage for validation and they, too, right on cue, began shrieking with piss-in-your-pants hilarity.

After a long while he finally caught his breath. He scanned the room. "Towel me," he said, and a flunky appeared wielding a fresh, fluffy white towel and began daubing and dabbing at the comedian's face.

From time to time Lewis's classes interfered with his nightclub appearances. To reconcile such conflicts he would fly the entire class to Las Vegas in a chartered jet. Glamour and excitement were attendant on these occasions to be sure, but so also was sickness. For Mr. Lewis considered himself something of an amateur pilot and from time to time insisted on occupying the cockpit and taking the stick.

On the several trips to Vegas we dove, looped, swooped, wheeoooped, and just generally downed Dramamine by the fistful. Once, after flying the plane directly through winding, twisting canyons near Lake Mead, Lewis emerged from the cockpit wearing a World War II kamikaze pilot's outfit, with leather earflaps, wire-rimmed glasses and wax buck teeth.

Sadly, in these, the waning days of Lewis's once-substantial popularity, his nightclub appearances were but thinly attended. Indeed, at the same time as his draw shriveled, he experienced the exquisite agony of observing his own son Gary's rock-and-roll act do turnaway business at the hotel on the strip immediately adjacent to the one where Lewis himself was performing. Various showbiz pundits suggested cynically that bringing our class to Vegas was the only way he could get bodies into the room.

Worst of all, Jerry became profoundly, perhaps even just a little drunkenly, pedagogical in what had once been a singing, dancing, joking, razzing, matazzing main-room act. His material was so old that the pages in the musicians' charts had grown yellow and brittle like parchment; their corners broke off when turned. Dying before a sparse crowd, he would lapse into his classroom schtick. "The filmic art, then," he would say, "explores, examines, and evaluates relationships, per se, and attitudes, as it were, rather than any mere spatial or experiential constructs. Per se. This is demonstrated, as it were, perhaps most clearly in my own cinematic filmic expression of creation, *The Errand Boy,* where frame sense and content and form meld and blend and combine into a unity that is mediate yet irrevocable."

"What is this crap?" patrons would holler from their twenty-eight-dollar seats. "Tell a friggin' joke, Cry-sakes. Make a funny noise. Fall on your ass, will you? Walk around funny. Insult somebody. Something. Anything." I found such moments quite simply excruciating. I tried to distract myself by thinking pleasant thoughts, but the situation was too depressing. I could think of nothing more appealing than wiping Pacifica's projectile vomit from the floor, walls, and ceiling.

"Maestro?" Lewis would say, turning to his musical director of a half-century, Lew Brown, and the band would hit a mellow riff. "Feelings . . ." Lewis would sing, "oh, whoa, whoah, whoahhh, feeeelings . . ."

20

MY OWN FEELINGS FOR Jerry Lewis evolved over the time
I knew him. From arm's-length skepticism bordering on contempt,
I moved to something very much like affection and even respect.

Was it also pity that I felt for him?

He was only in his forties, but his glory days were already behind
him and his professional life centered increasingly upon his weary,
tattered nightclub act, scattered TV talk-show guest host shots, and,
mainly, Good Works, most notably his campaign to conquer mus-
cular dystrophy. He had so peculiar a knack for offending people
that he was resented even for that.

Clearly, he had taken a liking to me. I expect it had something
to do with the fact that I never became a faithful soldier among the
army of yes-men perpetually surrounding him. I believe this explained why he soon adopted me as something of a confidant and
I suppose, frankly, I was dazzled.

There was no doubting the man's considerable talent and also his
discipline, even if the latter was—to be polite about it—inconsis-
tent.

The real problem was his taste.

And it wasn't that his taste was bad. The problem was he had no taste at all; taste simply did not exist in Jerry Lewis's art or in his life. It was as if those circuits had been shot off during the war.

And here lies the reason, I strongly expect, that despite flashes of brilliance he owned the ability also to shame and embarrass viewers even when they were watching him on TV alone in the privacy of their homes. He would commit an act so crude, take a turn so vulgar, as to cause a viewer to cover the eyes of his cat or guppy, to shield even the ottoman upon which he rested his feet in order to spare it the moment's humiliation.

In France, where the citizenry pretends to hate America but actually loves her, where the national pastime is to celebrate whatever it is that America most deplores, Jerry Lewis was embraced as a timeless superstar, a giant of cinema ranking with Chaplin, Eisenstein, and Kurosawa. In the late spring he was to be honored in a grand fête at the world-famous Paris Cinémathèque and, to my delight, he invited me to accompany him.

The turnout for the two-week retrospective certainly heartened Jerry Lewis. I enjoyed watching him enjoy himself. Good-sized crowds attended, and he got to answer questions about form and content in *Cinderfella,* to articulate the mimetic and metonymic development from, say, *Delicate Delinquent* to *The Ladies' Man,* and to discuss, additionally, diagetic iconography and syncretic influences in *Boeing Boeing* and *The Patsy.*

Most amazing of all, however, was that for the considerable excitement surrounding the event, the Hommage à Jerry Lewis was merely the second-hottest ticket on the Continent that spring. Far more grandiose was the excitement surrounding the discovery of a recently lost and underappreciated American film triumph called *Les Anges Terribles de l'Inferno.*

Custom-tuxedoed, standing on the pavement and counting the

house—enumerating each and every patron—as lines encircled the entire block several times were Slade Sloan, Perry, and Troy. Slade seemed remarkably thin. Perry had dark splotches on his face. After we'd recovered from the initial shock of running into each other so unexpectedly, and after we'd traded endless affectionate fives, hugged and kiss-kissed in that both-cheeks chichi French way, the boys dragged me to Maxim's—Dutch treat—and regaled me with tales of their European adventures.

Sucking down caviar at a buck an egg, Slade explained that "London was a bust. We thought we'd try Prague, but got on the wrong plane. You didn't get a telegram? We're a happening thing!"

"Veronica mentioned she'd heard from you," I vaguely recalled.

"And we owe it all to you, Stuart," Perry asserted.

"Me?"

"It's your script, isn't it?"

"So how come I get no screen credit?" I asked, squinting at the print ads they proudly unfolded and laid out on the table.

"Frog distributor removed it," Perry said, looking down woefully at his mirror-bright patent-leather pointy-toed shoes. "Talk to the French Cinéaste Guild."

"It's this 'auteur' crap," Troy volunteered. "To them the director is everything—actor, writer, cutter, grip, publicist, distributor, projectionist, popcorn popper, usher. All credit in this case goes, therefore, to Veronica."

"At least you keep it in the family," Slade told me.

"But that's what film is, isn't it?" I said. "Family. Screenwriters complain that so many people get between their script and the movie. But to me that's not film's downside but its greatest glory. A screenwriter gets to be a member of a vast, creative family of artists and craftsmen and businessmen struggling together with a shared purpose. To be part of that should give any artist cause to rejoice."

"That's what we love about you, Stuart," Troy said. "You're not caught up in all the ego-tripping that burdens lesser souls such as, for example, ourselves."

"We worried you'd object," Perry said, "but Veronica assured us you're above all that petty stuff."

"Veronica knew about this?" I asked.

"She didn't tell you? Likely she didn't want to burden you with unnecessary details."

"Blame France," Troy said. "They found our drecky little movie and turned it into an international phenomenon. What do they know? Guess who's their hero of heroes. Ready? Are you ready for this? Are you?"

I assured all assembled that I was ready.

"Jerry fucking Lewis!" he said and they all howled. "They love the guy. There's a freaking tribute going on here right now, do you believe it?"

I caught myself laughing along with my erstwhile roommates, pals, and collaborators over that uniquely ludicrous notion. But I knew that I was only playing along. And I suppose I was just a little ashamed, for failing to stick up not only for Jerry Lewis but also for myself.

21

UPON MY RETURN TO the States, bewildered by the European triumph that was and was not my own, I felt at once sated and hollow. I ate not at all and entirely too much; I slept all the time yet suffered also from insomnia.

Somewhere in the ocean of denial that preoccupied my consciousness, I knew the explanation had to be found in my cavalier surrender of writing credit on the movie. Try as I might to view the act as an ennobling good deed, the selfless generosity of a loving husband and faithful friend, I sank ever deeper into despair. Instead of pain I felt nothing. I thought I should be nourished, healed, blessed, one-with-the-universe, above the fray, all that. But during those fleeting moments when I felt anything at all, I was overcome mainly with mindless, numbing dread.

And dread was the best part of it. Far worse was the quiet, nagging rage that stole inexorably over my senses. Had I ever actually ceded the writing credit, I wondered, or merely let the subject grow cold and moot by default? And if this was the case, was I not the world's worst wimp?

I felt increasingly awkward with Veronica and seemed somehow to step back from the relationship just a bit. At first I thought I was simply depressed and reluctant to bum her out with my gloomy, dark moods. But in a remote corner of my consciousness I realized the prevailing sentiment was not so much sorrow as anger. I knew that I had to speak to the issue, but I couldn't find the time or the spirit or the will or the words to give voice to this newfound sense of betrayal.

Did Veronica even notice my withdrawal? Between the assignments she took to establish a career—here a commercial, there an educational film, news footage now and again for the local TV outlets—and mothering chores, perhaps she was willing to give me "my own space." Or maybe my retreat never even registered with her.

Whatever the case, I steeped myself in wholly bogus confidence that the darkness would soon lift. To the contrary, it steadily deepened. My sunshiny bright Southern California days were increasingly shrouded with a smog that was all my own.

In desperation, on a whim I drove all night through the desert to the closest corner of New Mexico, where I parked at a remote trailhead below lox-colored cliffs, which I awkwardly scaled. After some several hours I alighted, scraped and scratched, on a narrow ledge that held a crude and ancient adobe dwelling. I waited patiently beside the entrance, as I had been told was the custom, for what might have been another hour, or maybe it was two hours, or, on the other hand, perhaps it was mere minutes. The magical setting played tricks with time.

"Hello," I called out to nobody. "Hello?"

Nothing happened. A thought now occurred to me. I withdrew my wallet from my back pocket and placed it upon the worn stone that formed something of a stoop at the foot of the somber door. After a moment a scaly, bony hand reached out from the obscure interior, seized the wallet, and withdrew.

I continued to wait.

Nothing happened.

At last a scratchy voice croaked somewhere in the snapping, crackling wind. "Watch," it commanded.

I watched.

I watched the light change as clouds reshaped themselves across the sky. I watched the distant mountains, scanning them for something, anything: perhaps understanding, perhaps peace, perhaps liberation from the petty constraints of human ego that warped and stunted personalities for want of simple screen credit. I waited and watched, watched and waited.

Exactly nothing happened.

"Watch," the voice insisted yet again, and I carefully raked the horizon with my gaze, panning for life, death, either, neither, both. Again nothing at all happened.

"Watch!" the voice repeated with a slight urgency, and I heard myself complain aloud, "I'm watching, I'm watching."

"Watch!" was all the voice said.

And enlightenment all at once dawned. Fingers trembling, I worked the complicated clasp of my self-winding day-and-date Seiko, removed it from my wrist, and laid it on the stone pedestal before the door. Again the hand appeared; it whisked the watch into the dark interior.

And finally, after yet another pause that could have lasted seconds or weeks, there was a rustling from inside the solid yet ramshackle structure, and there emerged now a bent, aged figure with a face as crazed and craggy as the rocks themselves, wearing long gray Willie Nelson braids, wrapped in a wool-acrylic-blend Navajo-print blanket, bejeweled in turquoise and coral of Hopi design and Taiwanese manufacture.

He settled wordlessly onto the ground before me and crossed his legs Native American fashion.

At first he said nothing.

Then, after a long pause, he added nothing.

"Am I supposed to speak, or what?" I stammered.

The healer waited patiently and then, at last, said nothing.

"See," I offered, "I'm upset about my life and my wife and this credit thing. Is it sinful to desire credit for what's rightly one's own? Is that a sin? Is it? Am I a prisoner of ego? Is that it? Do I just learn to let go, or what?"

The hot, dry wind swept across the broad plane below and spiraled up from the mountain's base, raising tall tails of dust, minithunderheads that promised rain even if they were dry as bone.

"Does creativity exist for its own sake alone? Am I too hung up on status, property, possession, the whole modern, Western, industrial, linear mind-set? Is that it? That's got to be it, isn't it? Isn't it?"

The healer said nothing.

I contemplated his eloquent, articulate silence and wondered if I wasn't beginning to win a glimmer of understanding.

"What's the deal?" I asked. "Do I go with the flow? Let it all hang out? Do I rejoice in the success of my wife and friends and colleagues and cohorts and collaborators and comrades-in-arms?" I breathed slowly, heavily. "Do I embrace this success as my own? Is that the ticket? Is it?"

The shaman spoke not a word.

"Can't you even give me a clue?" I inquired earnestly.

The healer gazed in silence at the hills.

"Is it animal, vegetable, or mineral?" I asked at last.

The shaman cracked not a smile.

"Is it bigger than a motherfucking bread box?" I asked, anger rising in my throat, the stress now quite literally choking me. I scrambled for all the politeness I could muster and took a calming, cleansing breath. Then slowly, a word at a time, I reiterated, "Is it,

I say, bigger than a motherfucking bread fucking box?"

I should have been overcome by waves of remorse at having lost my composure, but now, quite miraculously, there was an unearthly fluttering of wings as a snow-white owl settled out of the heavens onto the broken beam supporting the adobe's humble roof.

"Hooo!" the owl called sharply.

"Dat dare," the healer said, curiously enough with a profound deeze-dem-doze Brooklyn bias, gesturing toward the bird, "concludes my remarks."

I was breathless with excitement and some indefinable something else that I took for true insight. "That's fantastic!" I gasped. "Incredible!" I whispered. "It now makes so much sense to me!" I asserted with passion and conviction and absolute, unchallenged, unchallenging certitude.

"I'm sorry," the healer said, looking at what had recently been my watch, "but dat's all de time we have for today."

22

STRETCH LIMOUSINES LINED THE block before the entrance to the Santa Monica Civic Auditorium, where kliegs probed the skies as if in search of stray Japanese bombers left over from World War II.

The only guy on our team with a real tux would have been me. The clerk at Tuxedo City had informed me that with shoes it was $87.50. When I explained politely that I intended not to purchase but merely to rent the garment, he nodded patiently, assuring me that he understood completely.

As for Troy and Perry, they wore polarized tuxedo-print cotton pullover shirts—one white-on-black, the other black-on-white—that they had not rented but purchased for only the tiniest fraction of the rental on my own After Six ensemble. Slade created quite a stir by appearing shirtless.

When at the last moment our sitter canceled, however, the evening's child care chores descended upon myself, and the tux suddenly became available. Characteristically, Veronica came charging into the house late, all out of breath, directly from the set of the instructional film on aircraft strut-riveting she was directing for Lockheed.

For a lark, she tried on the tux, and when she saw how smashing she looked, she promptly abandoned her custom-beaded gown to wear instead the loose-fitting tails and cummerbund, funkily cuffing the too-long black-satin-striped trouser legs, giving the whole outfit an arrogant, rock-and-roll, go-fuck-yourself elegance. The formal wear's masculine aspect provided the perfect field against which to accentuate her exquisite womanly loveliness. Never, not in all the years we'd been together, had she appeared more flat-out, full-tilt, all-out, full-bore sexy.

Thus suitably suited, Slade, Perry, Troy, and Veronica all waved to the fans and reporters as they made their way into the hall. And from the comfort of our living room, a daughter on either side, gazing at our flickering Zenith I watched them smile and nod. And I pretended that I genuinely preferred to spend the evening precisely this way. "Look!" I smiled, all brightness, turning first to one child and then the other. "There's Mommy!"

The girls fidgeted. "I wanna watch Big Bird," Pacifica protested.

Big sister Raynebeaux obligingly reached forward and switched channels, but I immediately switched back to the Oscar show. "Touch that dial again," I said sweetly, "and I'll cream you." The child burst into paroxysms of wailing that would not quit. If the truth be known, I welcomed the distraction, as it diverted my attention from the festivities and the detached sense of betrayal and exclusion that I surely must have felt.

And I was palpably ashamed of myself for the undeniable ripple of pleasure that ran through me when *Brutal Bad-ass Angels* failed to win any among the several Oscars for which it had been nominated. The nominations themselves, however, had generated sufficient interest in the project to win it a legitimate domestic distribution deal and, more important, to establish the reputations of the credited craftsfolk whose names shone upon the screen.

And damned if the movie didn't end up earning serious money. It was soon to become sufficiently remunerative as to cause two of our physician investors to be indicted for tax fraud. If both narrowly avoided jail, they were also virtually bankrupted, and the less expensively represented brought down five hundred hours of community service cleaning graffiti from city walls.

23

INDEED, ONE OF THE very same surfaces from which our physician investor had to remove graffiti was the cinder-block retaining wall fronting our own Echo Park digs. I passed him one morning as I made my way down the stairs on the way to my newly leased office. I was this very day moving in my brand-new, state-of-the-art Kaypro II, a computer that wrote screenplays.

They didn't call it that, of course. For some reason that would elude me into eternity, it was called a word processor. It had twin five-and-a-half-inch floppy disk drives and a screen that was almost as large as a postcard. It ran me nearly four thousand dollars in Jimmy Carter currency, and it was as cheap as that only because I knew a guy who knew a guy who knew a guy. Inflation was so rampant at the time that there were two price increases during the time I stood on line waiting to pay.

I loved best of all to watch the daisy wheel printer scan left to right, then right to left. The sucker could put out pages at a minute and a half each! I loved to unhook the tractor-drive perforated paper and separate the pages, one by one by one, watching them accumulate in a wispy but steadily increasing pile by my side.

Brutal Bad-ass Angels was now enjoying a wide release. And given its Scotch-tape-and-baling-wire budget, the profit participants (including the screen-credited artists, most notably Veronica) were actually seeing funds accrue from their net profit participation. It is said that in Hollywood true creative writing actually occurs in the accounting department; only when a movie earns so much money that the studio's comptrollers can't hide the proceeds from the Internal Revenue Service do any of the artists actually see some portion of the dollars due them.

And so it was with Veronica and, by association, also with me. We now had sufficient funds available for professional child care; Raynebeaux had already begun elementary school, and we were able to move her into one of the showbiz private schools of choice, the exclusive Harlake Eastwood.

House-husbanding chores were no longer necessary. Suddenly I was free to write full-time. Having children and child care in the house, however, disturbed irrevocably what had been the serenity of my study. I knew I needed off-premises premises, and therefore leased—with an option to buy—an industrial space, a loft, tucked neatly into one swirl of the cloverleaf exactly where the Santa Monica and Harbor freeways commingle on the southern edge of downtown.

Veronica's career was picking up steam. She was winning low-budget theatrical feature assignments for Roger Corman and American International Pictures and a handful of assorted Hollywood bottom feeders. I spent much time doctoring her projects—that is, revising the scripts before she shot them. But I also worked up my own pitches for television. Sitting in a comfy oaken swivel chair, parked before my funky, beat-up, previously owned cherrywood desk, which I'd liberated from the alley's overflowing Dumpsters, watched over as always by my faithful moosehead coatrack, I sketched out vague story lines for producers of sitcoms.

From time to time I'd traipse from my headquarters to one studio or another to pitch my pitch and schmooze up the troops. Sometimes I even made money doing this; far more often I did not. But the arrangements, the appointments, the chatter, the gossip, the driving, and the drive-on passes all had writing beat a mile.

". . . and they all go to the seashore," I concluded in just such a pitch at just such a studio—in this case CBS Television City in what passes for Hollywood but is actually Los Angeles—on a typical mid-morning of nonwriting.

"Love it!" the story editor responded. "That's a go for teleplay."

I was so familiar with rejection that the news fell on deaf ears. "Fair enough"—I nodded—"I've got another. Snooky dresses in drag for the school play and—"

"Didn't you hear me?" the executive interrupted. "I'm committing to the seashore bit."

"Really?"

"Really."

"Swell," I said, rising to leave, not quite believing I'd actually sold something.

"Wait," the producer protested. "What about the bit you came up with for Snooky? You said something about Snooky. He's in drag?"

"That's right," I agreed. "See, it's for the school play, and his daughter who's supposed to play Tinkerbell becomes ill, so he—"

"Fabulous!" the producer affirmed. "Call that a go, too."

"For true?" I asked. "Two episodes?"

"Can you handle it?"

"I can handle it," I assured him. "I can handle it." The room rocked, shook, rumbled, trembled just a bit. I figured a 2.5, tops.

"Got anything else?"

"But you've given me two assignments already," I said. "I can handle it," I assured him, "but I don't want to be greedy."

"Be greedy," he instructed me. "Who're you kidding? This is Hollywood. Wake up and smell the smog."

I hesitated a moment, and then I launched my third pitch in as many minutes. "Ziggy visits a consciousness-raising group and—"

"Hilarious!" The producer actually slapped his knee. "Timely. Contemporary. Relevant. All that."

"Another go?"

"Absolutely," he said, but then looked at me crookedly. "If you can handle it."

"I can handle it." After a moment I sheepishly inquired, just to be certain, "All three?"

The producer checked a list atop his desk. "Three? Don't you think you're getting a trifle greedy?" he said, as if none of the previous conversation had taken place. "Take two of the three."

"Agreed," I said quickly. "What's your pleasure? Which two shall I write?"

"You decide," he instructed me.

"Me?"

"Who else?" he said. "The butcher? The baker? The candle-fucking-stickmaker? You're the geek with the fancy-ass writing machine." Indeed, by this time my Kaypro II had been left at the curb and I worked on an IBM that had something called a hard drive with ten whole megabytes of memory self-contained. "And what difference does it make, anyhow? You haven't heard? We're canceled."

"Canceled?" I said, devastated. "Then why bother?" A frail temblor rattled the windows. Maybe a 2.0.

"The budget was committed months ago. We're funded for several more scripts, even if we don't shoot them. Still, they've got to be written. They'll never be produced, but the writers will be paid full scale. Can't you understand that?" A rippling motion passed through the room, very slightly agitating the ceramic figures on the executive's desk. "That had to be a 2.8," he said.

"Think so?" I asked him.

"Maybe even a flat-out 3."

"I go with your first guess. Maybe 2.9. Not more."

"You're not interested?"

"I'm interested," I told him.

"As long as you're sure you can handle it."

"I can handle it," I said. "I can handle it."

I strutted from the office with not one but two assignments in my pocket, and tipped the valet too much money when he delivered my VW. I drove up Highland and over the hill across Barham to NBC in Burbank.

The executive and his office could have been the same if you didn't look too closely; only the color of the leisure suit was different. "Paco dresses in drag for the school play and he—"

"Great!" the story boss said abruptly. "What else you got? You got anything else?"

I took a deep breath and said, "Hank visits a consciousness-raising group and—"

"Good stuff!" the man said. "I love them all."

"I can do both?"

"Are you serious? You're asking me for two slots?"

"Perhaps I'm being greedy."

"Hey, so what? It's Hollywood, right?" he said.

"Which of the two shall I do, then?" I asked him.

"Neither," he said. "Can't use you. Haven't you heard?"

"Show's canceled?"

"Worse," he said. "Picked up. We're renewed for next season, a definite twenty-six on the air."

"Congratulations," I said. And then, after what screenwriters too often describe as a beat, I said, "But why, then, can't I work for the show?"

"It's the only show the net's picked up, that's why. The boys upstairs are watching it closely." He reached into a mountain of papers on his desk, withdrew a blue-tinted memorandum, thrust it at me. "Some shithead do-good make-nice vice president has sent down this command. It's on blue memo paper but it's white."

"White?" I said.

"A white list. An inventory of approved, authorized writers for the show." I scanned some of the names: Edward Albee, William Inge, Arthur Miller, Thornton Wilder, Lillian Hellman.

To me they seemed unlikely to seek or accept an assignment on any second-season half-hour live-on-tape three-camera network television sitcom, but what did I know? "These writers have agreed to work for the show?" I asked.

"Of course not," the executive snapped. "For all I know, one or another of them is dead. This is some corporate officer's wet dream regarding creativity." He retrieved the memorandum from me and scanned it, shaking his head slowly. "The only motherfucker they left off this motherfucking list," he said at last, "is motherfucking Tennessee motherfucking Williams."

I took the list from him and scanned it. "Here it is," I said, pointing to the page.

"Ah, yes," the executive said, nodding. "What has he done? You know offhand who reps the guy?" he asked me, reaching for the phone. "Isn't he with Rick Alan at CMA?"

24

i DiD NOt KNOW who represented Tennessee Williams, though I was confident it was not Rick Alan at Creative Management Associates. Rick Alan happened to represent, among other writers, me; no matter how crazy Hollywood might be, I simply could not believe that Tennessee Williams and I had the same agent.

Alan had signed me and virtually anybody and everybody from film school who happened to drop by CMA's Ramada Inn of a headquarters on Beverly Boulevard near the Writers Guild. In practice, screenwriters themselves find their own assignments. Typically, they then turn the deal over to the agent, hoping he negotiates a contract for at least ten points more than they would have achieved solo. In this way the agency services are rendered effectively gratis.

This is why, notwithstanding the purported difficulty of finding representation, there is no shortage of agents who will in fact sign all comers. They expect quite rightly that from an army of clients trolling for jobs will emerge scattered commissions. Best of all, at least from the agents' point of view, they will have spent exactly no time shopping such writers and projects. Their only task is to collect the money.

Rick Alan was a youthful up-and-comer whose personality

synched perfectly with the profile then in vogue for bright new agents: neo-California sixties-seventies let-it-all-hang-out mellow combined with pit-bull tenacity and the ability smoothly, effortlessly to lie through broadly smiling teeth.

One glorious Southern California afternoon, a mere month into our relationship, Rick Alan was promptly and summarily fired for serving a client just a trifle too well.

And though I was blameless, it was also my fault, for I was that client.

Rick had actually found me a job, a rewrite of a story outline for a producer at MGM. Should he not have been roundly commended for securing employment for a client? Alas, Metro lay beyond Rick Alan's territory; in winning me the job he had trespassed upon a colleague's turf. Cheat on your taxes and your spouse, drive drunk, pillage and plunder, but if the San Fernando Valley's your beat, stay out of Culver City.

"A writer's job," crusty old USC film school writing instructor Gordon Michaels had asserted, "is to stay in his agent's face." I sought any excuse, therefore, to pop in on my rep. And on this particular day I happened to find Alan, amid the sweet and pungent pall of marijuana smoke that perpetually pervaded the offices, cleaning out his desk. "I've decided to move into production," he offered lamely.

" 'Decided,' my ass," scoffed my classmate, the underloved, overfed John Milius, another client in our USC-CMA family, watching Rick clear his shelves. " 'Production,' my ass. He's canned. Do what I just did, Stuart. Sprint to the end of the hall. They got a new guy and he's signing all of Rick's clients. Better hurry, though," Milius urged. "He's only accepting the first five hundred callers."

I made my way to the end of the corridor, sailed past secretary Sylvia Kaplan, and glided into Mike Medavoy's office.

The unevenly pleasant, just slightly stocky redhead had the phone jammed between his shoulder and ear as he toyed with the coiled cord. "We're close," he said idly either to someone at the other end of the line or—a not completely unknown agent's ploy—to nobody at all, merely a dial tone. "We're a hundred thousand apart." If it was a ruse, it won me completely.

And I would appreciate soon enough that Medavoy possessed the innate authority that requires no ploy.

25

it **WAS but A** few days later that Mike Medavoy rang me with orders to appear at Universal for a meeting with a recently appointed talent headhunter, Paul Statler. "They're looking at new writers," Mike told me. "At long last the studios have realized that nobody over the age of twenty-two goes to the movies. And at the same time they've come to recognize that nobody under the age of seventy-two works for the studios. So they've hired this kid—he's not even thirty; his nanny accompanies him to the office—to sniff around for writers who do not yet require an aluminum walker."

It is no small testimony to Medavoy's quiet power that I neglected to inform him that I had already met with Statler only a week earlier. That meeting had been arranged by USC's cinema chairman, Kevin Burns, who'd been approached directly by Universal in its search for fresh blood.

Certainly I should have told Mike about the earlier meeting, but instead, at the appointed day and hour I found myself riding the elevator to the fourteenth floor of Universal's sleek, glassy black tower, which is every bit as cozy as the monolith in *2001*. I was promptly ushered into Statler's office, but a single story below the aerie of the true power brokers.

In fulfillment of company policy, the chamber was furnished with general-issue French antiques, the pieces clearly on loan from the props department. The thin, dark young man swiveled from his view of the smog and smiled at me automatically but then, almost immediately, squinted with curiosity. "Don't I know you?"

"We're fast, fast friends," I said breezily, "practically roommates. We go back nearly a whole week already."

"One of the 'SC people." He nodded as the memory of our previous meeting came back to him. "But what are you doing here now?"

"I'm doing the same thing you're doing," I heard myself saying, "I'm loading my calendar with appointments. I'm driving to the studio. I'm parking the car. I'm riding the elevator. I'm sitting in your office and chatting. I'm posing and posturing as if I were a member of the professional film community. That's what I'm doing," I told Paul Statler. "What's significant," I added almost as an afterthought, "isn't what I'm doing but what I'm not doing."

"Oh? And what's that?"

"My job. Writing. I'm not writing." I stood outside myself, as if I were a third person at this meeting, eager to hear what I'd say next. "It's so much easier to cruise the freeways," I said, "to cop my drive-on pass at the studio gate, to sit here in an executive's office shooting the shit about the Dodgers or whatever, than to stay alone at my desk facing blank pages."

I knew I should shut up, but my mouth was in gear and I was powerless to stop talking. "Your own story is the same," I continued. "You're the studio's token Young Person. They give you a fancy-ass office. What they don't give you is a whit, a whisp, an iota, a shred, a shard, a speck, a fragment, a pale ghost of any genuine power. All you can do, therefore, is fill your calendar with appointments with young writers like myself, and together we benignly jerk each other around and squander our collective time."

I was immediately overcome by deep, dark regret for having chosen so clearly self-destructive a tack. What profit in disrespect?

"Please don't take offense," I pleaded in frantic retreat. "If I'm wrong, if you have any power at all, show it to me now. We had a perfectly pleasant chat a week ago. You said you liked me and my work." I paused and inhaled. "If you have an ounce of authority, if you have even merely a gram of authority, wield it now. Give me a freaking job."

Paul Statler looked at me long and hard, shaking his head slightly. He gradually unwound his lanky frame from the Louis Quatorze chair. Instead of knocking me to the ground as I richly deserved, he merely gestured ever so slightly with his chin. Clearly he was going to escort me personally to the door—perhaps all the way to the elevator—before instructing the guards never again to permit my shadow to darken the studio's Lankershim entrance.

Instead, he led me directly across the hall to the office of his immediate supervisor, an authentic fire-breathing Hollywood dinosaur who had known his fair share of filmland scandal. He had the too-good-to-be-true Hollywood name of Jennings Lang. Statler and I hung awkwardly in the entrance of Lang's inner sanctum.

As is typical of purportedly frenetic movie executives, Jennings Lang sat calmly at his immaculate desk, a script open before him but unseen by eyes looking not down but out the window at the mustard horizon. With not a word, with but the slightest cocking of his head, he bade Statler speak.

"See this arrogant snot-nose?" Paul Statler said, gesturing toward me as if it were necessary to do so. "Calls himself a writer. What have we got for him?" Statler's tone was so everyday as to suggest he was only asking for the key to the executive washroom.

"Give him this piece of shit to read," Lang responded. He shoved the script on his desk toward us. "We spent a quarter of a million on it, but it's got one problem: It sucks. If the guy can figure out a way to make this work," he said, without even once acknowledging my presence, "we'll give him a deal."

I drove to Art's Deli ("Every sandwich a work of Art"), five minutes up Ventura Boulevard, where it took me just about as long to read the script as to inhale the obligatory pastrami and not one but two bottles of Dr. Brown's Original Cream. The screenplay was a perfectly lifeless tale, essentially a chase, with lots of driving. The protagonist and his girlfriend drive here, there, everywhere; mobsters give chase, cops give chase, there's a romance—my member slept in my lap like a puppy throughout the most torrid love scene—and the couple endures a final, painful parting.

I knew exactly what could be done with this wretched story: nothing. I racked my brain for a handful of excruciating minutes and finally gave up. And at the precise moment when I surrendered, at that exact juncture where I quit trying, right there at Art's Deli of a weekday afternoon in the San Fernando Valley, the solution came to me in a flash.

It was but a single sentence. The words constituting that sentence are long lost to my feeble memory, but whatever they were is far less important than their cadence, their singsong rising-falling inflection, the rhythmic affect creating at once reassurance and sweetly dreadful dramatic stress.

I drove back to Universal and without pass or appointment strolled casually past the guard (hold your head high; go anywhere in Hollywood), rode the elevator to the fourteenth floor, smiled my way past Paul Statler's secretary, and waltzed directly into his office for the second time that hour.

"Ready?" I asked him.

What else could he do but tilt back in his chair, place both hands behind his head, and hear me out?

I stated my mellifluous sentence. I remember only that I used the word "relevant" a lot. And "relevant" just happened to be Hollywood's hot word that week.

Statler quietly reviewed the whole notion in his head. He rose and repeated the identical routine from the morning: He led me across the hall to Jennings Lang's office, where Lang sat yet again gazing out the window, yet again not reading yet another script that lay open upon his desk.

"He's got a solution," Statler told Lang. With both of them now staring at me, I realized it was once again my turn to speak. I took a breath, then launched anew my fast few phrases.

"I like it," Jennings Lang said.

"We have a deal?" I inquired.

"We have a deal," Lang said, and my spirit took flight, but he just as quickly added, "As long as Emm-Oh-Double-You will finance."

"Emm-Oh Who?" I asked.

"Movie of the Week," Lang explained. "M.O.W. Get it?"

"No," I reported honestly.

"We got a new guy here doing a new thing," Lang explained. "The guy is Sid Sheinberg. The thing is Movie of the Week. Original movies made expressly for TV. If Sid will finance it out of his budget, we have a deal."

Lang rose from behind his desk. The three of us rode the elevator down some several floors and emerged in a corridor indistinguishable from any other. We came to a closed door before which paced a nervous man. "Hello, Stuart," the man greeted me with what seemed like forced brightness. I instantly recognized my writing teacher from the USC film school, Gordon Michaels himself.

"Hi, Professor Michaels," I managed to say.

Ignoring me and my mentor, Lang growled at a secretary, "He there?"

"On the phone," Gordon Michaels answered for her.

"On two phones," the secretary said, glancing at the glowing buttons on her telephone desk set.

"I'm hoping to find a thirty-second slot," Michaels asserted. "I'm confident if I can just pitch Sid this notion, he'll agree we ought to close a development deal forthwith. Otherwise," he said in what was clearly a crude attempt to impress Jennings Lang, who was not even pretending to listen, "I'll take this up the block to CBS Theatrical Films."

There was no escaping the irony in Lang seizing the knob as he did and, right before Michaels's eyes, sweeping myself—the mere teaching assistant, the goddamned protégé—past him and into the presence of the very honcho who was presently refusing to grant him audience.

This unlikely trio—Lang, Statler, I—stood in the entrance, the door still partially open behind us, as Michaels all the while bobbed and feinted in the background, struggling to make eye contact with the immovable Sheinberg. Indeed, as the secretary had informed us, the executive vice president spoke simultaneously into not one but two phones. Recognizing Lang, Sheinberg said to both receivers, "Hang on a second," and then, resting each on a shoulder, with a quick nod he indicated that Lang should speak.

Lang looked to me.

Nobody said anything and I realized after a moment that it was my turn to give voice to something, anything. I swallowed hard, grabbed a quick breath, and for the third time in as many minutes launched my eight-second pitch. Sidney Jay Sheinberg nodded. Jennings Lang returned the nod, held the door open, ushered Statler and me from the office, and closed the door behind us, leaving Sheinberg alone again to confront his telephones.

"Sid?" Gordon Michaels called anxiously through the closed door. "Can I talk to you for just half a minute? Can I, Sid? Sid?"

Did I have a deal? Did I not?

My phone rang as I walked in the door at home. "It's not gonna work out," Mike Medavoy told me.

"They don't want me?"

"They want you."

"Then what's the problem?"

"They want you for seven years."

"Seven years?"

"They want to put you on staff for seven—count 'em, seven—years. Renewable at their option, not ours, every six months. Exclusive. They can tie you up till you're thirty." Thirty! I'd require a pacemaker and an IV drip.

"And in the meantime I can't work for any other studio?"

"Or network or independent production company."

"And what do they propose as compensation?" I inquired as casually as I could. In truth, the thought of being "tied up" by a major Hollywood studio didn't strike me on its face as a wholly unacceptable proposition.

"Five hundred bucks a week for the first six months," Medavoy explained with obvious disappointment. Had I heard him right? To me, at that time, five hundred dollars represented a veritable fortune all by itself, never mind five hundred dollars a week. "And there are escalators."

"Escalators."

"Seven hundred per for the second six months, then nine, eleven, and then it jumps to fifteen flat and then two grand for the duration. As long as you're not working."

"Not working," I said.

"When you're actually on assignment, of course, you'll receive Guild scale plus an escalating bump, ten points, twenty, and so on until it's scale times two and a half."

"I see," I lied once again to my agent.

"Completely unacceptable," he said. "Right?"

"Right," I said. "Right?"

"Right," Mike said with finality.

"Right?" I asked him.

"It's the way the business does itself in," Medavoy explained patiently. "It devours its young. It pretends to want to develop new talent, but what it really desires is only to stifle art and artists, to suffocate creativity with old-fashioned long-term obligations left over from another era."

If anybody wants to suffocate me, I told myself but not Mike Medavoy, let them do it with five hundred crisp ones every week. With bumps, perks, escalators, and whatever else, all that stuff he had babbled. But what I said to Medavoy was: "So we kiss them off?"

"No," he said. "I'll try to talk some sense into them. Meantime, you just stand by."

I just stood by. I just stood by for one day and then another, and then I just stood by for one week and then another.

And then I just stood by for another week after that.

26

hollywood is the one place on earth where you start at the top and work your way down. Here I'd had a genuine offer of employment from a major studio for what struck me as riches beyond imagination. And what had I reaped? Frustration and despair.

And just about the time I'd surrendered all hope, the phone rang. "Any progress?" I dared ask Mike Medavoy.

"Worse than no progress," he said. "You've heard of the Cahuenga Pass? This is the Cahuenga Impasse. The good news is I've gotten them to throw in an office."

"I already have an office, Mike."

"I know that, and they know that, and that is why they've agreed to it—because it has no value, don't you see?"

I saw.

"What happens in a case like this sometimes," Medavoy went on to explain, "is the principals meet and talk to each other. Universal's negotiator, Peter Rutersdorf, wants to meet with you personally in order to explain the company's position. You don't have to do it if you don't want to. Do you think you can handle it?"

The meeting with Rutersdorf was scheduled for three in the afternoon early the following week, and I orchestrated my whole life around it. I ate, slept, and breathed Universal Pictures Corporation. I perpetually planned alternate routes to the studio. Our Echo Park bungalow was but ten minutes from Universal by any number of routes. Not at the appointed hour then, but with ninety minutes to spare, I slipped behind the wheel of my faithful Volks.

Veronica was just pulling up to the house with Raynebeaux in tow. She had invited the entire second grade on a class trip to watch her direct her first major network TV series episode, the fourth installment of *Snip,* a *Shampoo* knock-off starring David Brenner as a prissy hairdresser. Given the bright, fresh concept, plus the proven staying power of a giant talent such as Brenner, there could be no doubt the show would dominate Tuesday nights for years to come and make everyone forget *All in the Family.*

I chose the scenic route through Griffith Park, past Crystal Springs, the golf course, zoo, Forest Lawn Drive to Barham, then over the hill to Lankershim and straight through the studio gate. At least that was the plan. There was, however, an unanticipated problem: The park was ablaze.

Old St. Anne was blowing her fool heart out. The dry, stiff, searing, ionized air raged at gale force. I entered the park at Los Feliz and was soon passed in both directions by howling, screaming fire trucks. As I cruised Zoo Drive, cutting directly through the golf course, the stands of eucalyptus lining both curbs were alive with prancing, dancing flames.

It was straight out of *Bambi.*

Just the other side of Travel Town, I came to a dead halt behind emergency vehicles and was finally rerouted by cops, sheriffs, and fire marshals to God alone knows where. I snacked internally upon my stomach lining as I waited endlessly behind ambulances and tow trucks. Perishing in smoke and flame frightened me not a whit; my true panic derived solely from the prospect of arriving late for the meeting with Rutersdorf.

And indeed, by the time the studio security officer, the legendary Scotty, waved me through the main gate, I was five full minutes tardy. Breathless, ruined and wrecked, gasping and wheezing and panting, sooty sweat streaking my face, ashes smudging my brand-new-for-the-occasion linen-white canvas Keds, I sprinted to Rutersdorf's secretary's desk.

"Mr. Rutersdorf is running just a trifle late," the woman informed me most politely. "Do you mind waiting just a bit?"

Here should have been a welcome opportunity to catch my breath and put on my game face. Nevertheless, once again, as if I were standing outside myself listening to my own words, I heard my voice exclaim, "Late? A little late? Do I mind waiting?" I pointed east through the panoramic glass wall where smoke blackened the sky just beyond the lot. "I drove through Dante's motherfreaking Inferno to arrive here in a timely fashion," I said. "The least Peter could do is be here at the appointed hour."

The secretary, instead of directing me to go straight to hell as I surely deserved, turned abruptly and fled. Within moments she returned accompanied by a guy who looked as if his name could only be Peter Rutersdorf. He was a benign, bespectacled, slightly goofy, good-natured gentleman in a straighter-than-straight business suit.

"I'm sorry to be late," he said, ushering me into his office.

"I should hope to Christ you're sorry," I sputtered. The only thing more appalling than my behavior was Universal's toleration of my behavior. Rutersdorf talked economic gobbledygook and I half listened, half gazed out the window at the continuing drama across the hill in Griffith Park, my attention fading in and out like a short-wave radio. "And so the question is," I was suddenly aware of Rutersdorf saying, "whether or not the movie business is going to survive."

"Let me set your mind at ease right away," I told him bluntly. "The leisure-time and entertainment industry—including movies—is going to survive. And grow. And flourish as never before. The question is: Will Universal Studios be part of that rich, bright, productive, prosperous future?"

"Exactly," Rutersdorf said, at once guarded and patronizing. "Which is why we feel it's imperative we help young talent."

"Don't help young talent," I said. "Let young talent help you." That Peter Rutersdorf did not eject me bodily from his office forever diminishes his stature in my eyes. "You posture as if the studio wishes to act selflessly," I said. "You claim you want to offer a new artist an opportunity, but the only opportunity is for that very same artist to become an indentured servant under the precise style of exploitation against which this nation rebelled now nearly two hundred years ago."

This nation! Two hundred years! I was flying on instruments.

And I was struck by the incongruity of my chest-beating, my running at the mouth. How did I reconcile such assertiveness before this powerful studio executive with my craven inability to demand from my own wife proper screen credit that was properly due me?

Rutersdorf was rendered quite thoroughly silent. "This is the way the business does itself in, devours its young," I ranted, just to fill the silence, believing Mike Medavoy's words as I recited them. "It pretends to want to develop new talent, but what it really desires is only to stifle art and artists, to suffocate creativity with old-fashioned long-term obligations left over from another era."

Marinating in the muck of self-satisfaction, I soon found myself affixing my signature to documents, multiple copies of the contract, and also initialing as directed here, here, and also here, plus Appendix A, whatever that was, blithely consenting to precisely the studio agreement containing every limitation I had nailed so eloquently only moments earlier.

27

DESPITE MY ARROGANT ATTEMPTS to dissuade Universal from hiring me, despite my faithful representative's enlightened caveat, I found myself now suddenly a slave to a major studio. Still, as writers will admit only to other writers, there is no experience more mellowing than swapping language for dollars. We get paid, after all, for what others are scolded for: daydreaming. If the truth be known, there breathed not a clam happier than I.

I was now on payroll but not expected to work on the rewrite until an outline was approved, I never knew quite by whom. There was no one in particular to whom I was to report. Despite my apparent good fortune, despite the fact that my major-studio gig made me the envy of all my film-phony pals, I sensed a veil of darkness descending.

I told myself that I was as free as a bird. But are birds really free? They soar, and it all looks so easy. We figure they're having the most fabulous time, swooping, looping, gliding, reveling in the glorious view. But aren't they really hard at work, desperate to scrounge up a seed, to scavenge a maggot, a mealworm, a beetle?

Of course I abandoned my own office downtown, taking with me to Universal only my moosehead coatrack. There was no way I could resist driving to the studio each day to park in my studio parking place, to sit in my studio office just across the hall from Jackie Cooper's suite, to talk on my studio phone. I arose daily at noon's early light, arriving at the lot just in time for a long, leisurely lunch; it was not a bit unusual for me to work at my desk well past three-thirty in the afternoon.

Being waved through the gate by Scotty without even having to pause for identification—my newly contrived, rancid good-guy smile was all the ID required—and pulling into my space, which was immediately next to that of, so help me God, Paul Newman, were details I did not fail to share with my friends and, even better, my enemies, and also no small number of strangers. I told the mailman, the supermarket checker, the clerk at the Motor Vehicle Bureau that I just happened to be on my way to my office at Universal Studios where I just happened to be under contract as a writer, that's right, Universal, writer, where I just happened to have the parking space next to that of Paul Newman.

That's right. Newman. Paul. Newman.

Sometimes, just for a lark, I would pop into a convenience store to purchase a pack of gum that I did not need, simply to enlighten yet another lucky soul—somebody, anybody, a cat, a dog—as to my newfound stature.

Once I visited the campus at USC in order to relate casually to my now former film school professors that I was on staff at Universal. This news was greeted not with congratulations but derision, not with good wishes but palpably jealous resentment. I had "sold out." I was "copping to the establishment." It must be a dreadful experience, I mused, to teach at a prominent film school and observe one's students move on to success dwarfing one's own.

And week after week after week I did all these things and more.

What I did not do was write.

Finally, perhaps after a month, maybe a couple of months, exhausted and bored beyond description, I sat myself down before my studio typewriter and in desperation actually sketched out a broad overview of the rewrite for which I had been hired. More than vaguely satisfied, now with several pages of outline to guide me, I felt ready to dive into a fully fleshed-out first draft.

But instead of just jumping in and writing, I decided that it would be brilliantly politic for me first to consult with somebody. Anybody. Eventually I learned that Paul Statler was now technically the producer of this project. As he was among a handful of people in the movie business with even less experience than I, there could be little doubt he would, of course, grant me his swift and eager approval.

But on reviewing my outline, Paul announced that he had his own notions as to how the tale should go, and more than a few suggestions regarding what he deemed to be improvements over my particular approach here, there, and elsewhere.

For the sake of strategy alone, I spent another couple of weeks diddling with words until I had an outline that I was wholly confident would win me both my producer's approval and, there could be no question about it, an Oscar. I admit I played around—only for a couple of days—framing my acceptance speech, never getting much past the "I wish to thank the members of the Academy" part.

When I presented the revised outline to Statler, however, both he and I were rudely disappointed, he with the outline, me with his reaction to the outline. He liked this aspect and that one, but he was troubled here, there, and in another place. This character seemed strong, but needed to be weak. That character appeared weak, but needed to be strong.

In my heart, I believed I was quite ready to begin writing a first draft. To review the tale again and again seemed antithetical to any useful purpose.

Nevertheless, day after day I sat alone in my office, scratching with a pencil against a yellow legal pad, occasionally even typing a few lines before throwing away the page, just generally making myself miserable. Generous compensation aside, big fancy movie studio aside, parking place next to Paul Newman's aside, I became quite familiar with that inevitable companion of all true writers: deep, dark despair.

Every twenty-two minutes, like clockwork, I heard the tour tram's public address system crackle to life as the little orange-and-white train snaked past and around my building. There was an amorphous, echoey spiel, which would finally come into focus with ". . . and if all the outtakes were laid end to end they would stretch . . ." before quickly retreating beyond intelligibility. The studio tour was then a new enterprise at Universal, but it was already so successful that film crews—perpetually obsessing about unemployment—joked that no matter how thin production schedules might become, Universal would always have at least one movie shooting on the lot, if only to have something to show the tour.

Myself, instead of writing, I took to wandering aimlessly around the vast acres of rugged back-lot wilderness, a wondrous anomaly smack in the middle of a bustling world-class cosmopolitan center. Eventually a major portion of that same acreage would be occupied by Steven Spielberg's sprawling Amblin compound. But back then there were running creeks in deep woods populated by real possums, skunks, coyotes, and even deer. I suspected a lost Native American tribe would one day emerge from the thicket.

In all the years that have passed I've never discovered what outtakes the studio tour guides were talking about, nor, if laid end to end, to where in the world they might finally stretch.

28

MY bACK-lot hikes SOON slammed to an abrupt halt.

"Freeze," a voice squawked over a bullhorn, "and place your hands behind your head."

I turned to greet a vehicle, its red-and-blue lights flashing. The doors flew open and a uniformed pair of what appeared to be law enforcement officers approached. "You have the right to remain silent," they volunteered, adding that if I chose to speak, anything I said could and would be used against me in a court of law.

From the uniforms I was quickly able to determine that these were, in fact, studio guards. Drape a uniform on a wino, pay him a buck sixty-five in Jimmy Carter dollars, and you've got a studio security officer. They had taken me for a terrorist or, even worse, a tourist on the lam from the tram.

The guards radioed studio security headquarters, which in turn telephoned the personnel department, which verified my legitimacy. I was escorted personally to my office, where the phone was ringing. "You're trespassing on the backlot?" Paul Statler asked me.

"They've already called you?"

"Likely they've already called Mr. Wasserman himself," Paul said, "to say nothing of the California Air National Guard. What are you doing skulking about the lot?"

"Thinking," I responded. "Dreaming. I'm a writer. I can't be cooped up in this office all day and at the same time invent free-wheeling fantasies."

"Relevant freewheeling fantasies," Statler said.

"I need to get out into the daylight from time to time. It's a crime for a writer to take a stroll?"

"It is no crime," Statler reassured me. "It is merely a violation of insurance regulations, union covenants, and actuarial schedules. Tell you what. You can't wander freely around the back lot, but you can ride around in a limousine. I'll assign you a car and a Teamster to chauffeur you."

"I want to walk."

"I'll assign you a limo and a Teamster and a fire marshal," Statler countered, "and you can walk around the lot as they drive quietly and discreetly a short distance behind you."

Idle artistic contemplation did not strike me as congruent with a lurking car, Teamster, and fire marshal. I politely declined the offer and vowed to confine myself to the office until the damned outline was ready.

To this end, I started reporting to work a whole hour earlier each day, sat diligently at my desk, and avoided reading the trades. But still I did not write. What I did was stare out the window across the narrow alley at the broad, flat face of Stage Twelve. If I did not accomplish anything on the script, I became better acquainted with that west wall of Stage Twelve.

The wall, like all Universal's soundstages, was coated with thick raked plaster that was painted a plain, dull grey. One could clearly see that while still wet it had been combed in such a manner as to create subtly swirling patterns of parallel ridges and valleys, a stucco corduroy.

Affixed high atop the wall was a crook-necked streetlight. I found myself spending long hours watching the shadow cast by the fixture upon the alley floor, tracking its daily path across the pavement to the bottom of the wall. I don't doubt that I tracked that shadow far more closely than any mental health professional would have deemed appropriate.

For no reason at all, I came regularly to celebrate the precise moment each day when the blurred, soft, leading edge of the fixture's shadow first brushed the wall, and I noted also, as the season wore ever onward, that this moment arrived each day just a hair later. In particular, I was amazed that it took the shadow nearly all morning to make its way across the pavement, but only thirty-eight minutes and a fraction to move the much greater distance from the wall's bottom to its top.

Confused by this apparent contradiction, I soon came to realize it had to be explained by the abrupt change in angle. The wall was, of course, turned ninety degrees against the alley floor. Once the shadow hit the wall, it had the same amount of time to travel a far greater distance. It appeared, therefore, to move more quickly.

One day, watching that accursed shadow, I was able to experience what I took to be a life-changing insight. I sat, as always, quiet and still as Stage Twelve itself, staring unblinkingly at the shadow as it concluded its foreshortened journey across the alley floor. Then once again it began to slither up the wall.

Concentrating most precisely upon the shadow's top edge, I suddenly realized that, if I stared carefully enough, with my naked eye I could actually see the shadow's motion, like the minute hand of a clock. Right before my very eyes, it moved from a stucco ridge, flowed down through a minivale, then moved on to the next ridge a millimeter away. Then up, down, up, ridge to valley, valley to ridge, the patch of lightlessness progressing ever higher up the wall.

It dawned on me that what I observed before my very eyes was the globe revolving on its axis.

I was positively dizzy with excitement.

My heart aflutter, my breath rasping in my throat, I leaped from my chair, raced into the corridor, and pounded on Jackie Cooper's door. He was producing and starring in a half-hour pilot about a child psychologist. His secretary, bright, blond, blue-eyed Diane, peeked out at me. "You gotta see this!" I gasped. "Get Jack!"

"He's in a meeting," Diane said, pointing to the closed interior door.

"Never mind no meeting." I barged into the receptionist's office and yanked open the inner door, startling Jackie Cooper and his production manager, with whom he was arguing budget.

"Everything okay, Stuart?" Jackie Cooper asked me cautiously.

"Come quick! Quick! You're not gonna believe this!" I babbled very much in the manner of a maniac.

I raced back past Diane, out into the hall, and into my own office, where I ran directly to the window and stared out at the glorious image of the fixture's shadow on Stage Twelve. I turned in triumph to the door, expecting to see Jackie Cooper. Instead, there was nobody.

After a moment, three faces popped into view at odd angles within my door frame: Jackie Cooper, his secretary, Diane, and the production manager. The expressions on those faces were identical: confusion and concern.

"Don't you see?" I whined, my eyes popping, my arms flailing wildly toward the flat-finish gray wall of Stage Twelve.

In perfect synchronization, all eyes panned slowly from me to the window. And, clearly, all three faces missed the significance of what was revealed. My voice, fractured with excitement, cracking like an adolescent's, explained: "The earth! Don't you see? It's moving! Turning! The earth! It's turning!"

29

tREMbliNg, i SEARChED EACh face for affirmation but observed instead only wary discomfort, even pity. Soon enough the faces nodded, first to each other and then to myself, and now one at a time they departed.

Alone in my office, then and there I knew I had played too, too long with the outline. After all the many weeks of struggling and suffering, my course seemed now splendidly clear: go for a walk.

And so I partook once more of a contemplative, lonely stroll around the lot. Or, I should say, the stroll was as contemplative and lonely as possible when one is stalked by a gleaming white stretch limo piloted by a Teamster and, just as a bonus, a uniformed studio fire marshal in a studio security car who would nip now and again at a bottle of cough syrup.

As if all that were not quite enough, when our minicaravan crept through the medieval European village street and moved into East Harlem, as we turned onto the turn-of-the-century Midwestern American Main Street, just past the old *Psycho* exterior, I heard behind me the all-too-familiar strain: ". . . the outtakes laid end to end would stretch . . ."

I turned to observe a studio tour tram, jammed with visitors, making its way past Generic Contemporary Suburban Street, running parallel to our own path. With all the traffic, I might as well have been on the center divider of the Pomona Freeway.

I was grateful, therefore, to see a teenage girl suddenly bolt the tram. In what appeared very much a practiced move, she hit the faux cobblestones running. The tour guide was a clean-cut Californian perhaps twenty-two years old, sporting a name tag ("Michael") on his pale yellow MCA blazer. Before he could intercede, the girl sprinted a short distance along the meandering street and vanished between some clapboard and plywood false fronts.

I say I was grateful, because both the fire marshal and the limo-driving Teamster lit out after the fugitive and I found myself now, therefore, blissfully alone. Given the serenity engendered by solitude, presumably I could now chart a strategy regarding the damned and damnable outline. Again, I wondered if I shouldn't simply ignore my so-called producer and just jump into the script itself.

Perhaps a few moments passed, perhaps it was a half-hour, but within that time I had resolved to become my own master and live and write as I pleased, to hell with Black Tower authorizations and approvals: Then, suddenly, turning onto the otherwise deserted Western Street, I observed a sight that filled me with authentic horror.

A frail figure, clearly the young girl who had fled the tour tram, stood atop the hangman's scaffold, carefully and deliberately placing the noose over her own head. Now, with her foot, she took a swipe at the trapdoor release lever a short distance away.

"Wait!" I yelled, and raced toward her. "Don't!"

All the while she flailed with her toe in an effort to catch and trip the lever.

"No!" I shouted as I raced for the scaffold.

But at the very moment I arrived, she succeeded in nudging just enough of the lever's handle to trigger the device and collapse the panel beneath her feet. Her body dropped the short distance the rope allowed. Her head snapped. Her body jerked and then swung solemnly, morbidly, up and back, her toes dangling mere inches above the scrubby ground.

Three at a time I bounded the scaffold steps and seized her beneath her shoulders, hauling her upward, trying to alleviate the rope's tension.

"What the heck are you doing, mister?"

She was alive! "I don't care how bad it is," I said to her, still hoisting her body as best I could with one hand, while at the same time the other grasped frantically at the knot that secured the noose. "There's got to be a better way," I assured her, breathless.

"It's okay," she said. "Really. See? I'm all right. See? See?"

She pointed to a clear plastic body harness draped under her arms, around and beneath her shoulders, and behind her back. "Special effects," she explained. "I worked it up in my dad's garage in Van Nuys."

She yanked on a loose cord, and the noose instantaneously sprung free of her neck. She led me to the scaffold's edge and down the steps to the dusty dirt street.

Awkward, gawky as she was, with a mouthful of orthodontia, there was something hypnotic in her soft hazel eyes. "Who are you?" she asked. "Are you anybody important?"

"No," I said. "Are you?"

"I'm going to be," she said.

"A glamorous movie actress, no doubt."

"Hell, no," she said. "A director."

Just now there was the sound of a motor and a man's voice called out, "Anybody there?" The fire marshal's vehicle eased into view as he prowled the lot, searching for the little trespasser. "Hello? Hello? Come out! Hello?" She looked up at me, quietly pleading, and put her finger to her lips, urging me to silence.

Of course I should have turned her in then and there. For reasons I would not come to understand until years later, I did not merely acquiesce; I actively colluded with her. We ducked into the phony entrance of a phony gold-assay office, hiding out until not one but several security cars rolled down the street, flashers flashing.

"My name is Ginger Kenton," she offered plain as day, once the cars were gone, as if we were merely chatting at a party. "I crash the studio two, three times a week, wander around, learn the ropes."

"Ropes, indeed," I said, gesturing toward her neck.

"How'd you get in?" she asked me.

"I work here," I explained.

"I figured that out already," she said. "I mean the biz. How'd you get into the motion picture business?"

I thought for a moment. And then I said, "Film school."

"Film school?" she asked, incredulous. "They teach movies in school?"

Now there was the sudden dull repetitive thumping of a helicopter's rotor and, in a flash, a big whirlybird settled onto the Western Street, kicking up plumes of dust. Armed guards leaped from the chopper and approached the ersatz gold-assay office. "Freeze," an official voice barked over a bullhorn. "You are under arrest. You have the right to remain silent. In the event you do choose to speak . . ."

I was beginning to lose count of how many times I'd heard my rights read to me since coming to California.

I turned to face Ginger Kenton, to reassure her, but she was gone. I found myself alone except, of course, for perhaps a dozen private law enforcement personnel in varying uniforms and varying degrees of sobriety.

30

ALONE AGAIN IN MY office, I knew I had played too, too long with the outline and, authorized or not, the moment had arrived to start scripting.

Uncharacteristically, I remained at my station clear through to dawn, missing Raynebeaux's performance as Tinkerbell in her second-grade class's production of *Peter Pan,* and also the wrap party for her mom's low-budget theatrical feature, a project she'd taken over after the original director collapsed on location in a cocaine fit. When I shambled wearily from the lot in the earliest light, I left twenty-six pages of an actual draft stacked neatly on my desk.

But how to handle Statler, whose approval I still required? That thought was deferred for what I planned to be a couple of days but soon turned into some weeks.

The script grew steadily longer. With the draft nearly completed, one day, quite by accident, I ran into Statler at the studio newsstand.

"You notice I haven't been rushing you," he told me truthfully. "I stand on what I said: Take as much time as you need." And having said that, he promptly asked me precisely when I imagined I might have something resembling a revised outline. Instead of formulating some cagey response, I committed a fatal Hollywood error: I told the truth. I confessed that I had already written a substantial portion of the script, some eighty-five pages. My too-breathy overeager voice pronounced this in such a manner as to suggest it could be regarded only as welcome news.

But from the unmistakable disappointment that crossed his face, it should have been clear that, though not yet even fully written, the script was already dead in the water. What need for Statler even to read the pages? This whippersnapper writer, barely out of film school, goes off half-cocked and, without authorization, proceeds to a draft. Who needs to read the draft to know it's lousy?

Naively, however, I clung as writers do to the belief that the pages themselves would save me. Once he actually read the pages, Statler would see the wisdom in what I had done. There could be no escaping the brilliance of such pages. My course was clear: finish the script as quickly as I could.

And one week later, cockily confident, I handed the completed draft to Statler's secretary. The door to his office was partly open, and I could hear a male voice engaged in a telephone conversation. "Is he there?" I cautiously asked the secretary.

"Do you mean Paul Statler?"

"Precisely."

"No longer with the studio." Her phone rang and she was promptly distracted. In Hollywood, it is acceptable behavior for flesh-and-blood folks to stand in line behind souls on the telephone. I quietly extricated the script from the secretary's grasp and made my way to the door of what used to be Paul Statler's office. I knocked gently and the door gave way to the pressure of my knuckles.

Engaged in an energetic exchange on the phone, a young man twisted and twirled the spiral phone cord. The fellow seemed familiar to me, and after a moment I recognized him as the now-former tour guide whose badge had read "Michael." Perhaps a month had passed since young Ginger Kenton had bolted from his tram. He concluded his conversation and hung up the phone.

"Hi," he said, extending a long arm across the desk. "I'm Mike Ovitz. I'm Paul Statler's replacement." As I shook his hand, he began to unbuckle his belt. "What's that?" he said, pointing to the script in my hand.

"It's a screenplay," I explained. He stepped out of his pants and began to unbutton his shirt.

"No, it's not," he said.

"Not?"

"A screenplay," Michael Ovitz told me. "Not."

"It's not a screenplay?

"Correct. It is a vehicle."

"Vehicle?" I asked him as he stepped from his shoes. He now began pulling on a white tae kwon do outfit, one of those loose and bulky canvas costumes worn by martial arts dudes. "Scripts, screenplays, scenarios they no longer exist."

"No?"

"No. There used to be movies and screenplays and actors and directors and producers. But that's Hollywood history."

"And today?"

"Today there are only packages based on vehicles containing elements." He seized a thick plank of wood and thrust it at me. "Here. Hold this."

I performed as I was instructed. In another moment his hand sailed through the air at warp speed. Before I knew what had happened, the plank was gone from my outstretched arms and residing at my feet as a pile of sawdust.

"You want to succeed in this business?" Michael Ovitz asked me. "Get out of the studio. Studios are old news. Writers? Directors?

Actors? Producers? Executives? That's yesterday. Never mind yesterday. That's a week ago Thursday. That's the silent era. Today it's agencies and packagers. That's the route to take. Myself? I'm here for five minutes. This development job is merely a cover for my true job search, an entry-level position at a talent agency. Once I'm there, I plan to steal all their best clients and form my own agency. Here." He handed me a slab of green Vermont marble. I held it aloft and in a moment, after a flurry of flailing, flashing hands, the slab was gone and I stood amid a pile of pebbles and powder. "You want power in the movie business? You have to control the elements: actors, directors, producers, writers. And you have to control the product that the writers produce: vehicles for the other elements."

I left my script on the corner of his desk and departed.

The very next morning I drove to the studio to be greeted warmly as always by Scotty, faithful at his post guarding the main entrance on Lankershim Boulevard. But as I pulled up to my parking place I knew immediately there was something amiss. Paul Newman's name continued to mark the concrete curb directly next to my own. My name, however, had been painted over in pure, gleaming white.

I proceeded to C Building and climbed the single flight to my office to be greeted by the same phenomenon: My name was gone from the door. Nevertheless, the key successfully negotiated the lock. Inside, my office was still my office, and through the window there was still the view of Stage Twelve's west wall with the shadow of the streetlight crawling across the fine field of raked stucco.

Calmly, I lifted the phone, requested an outside line, dialed Universal Studios, and asked to be connected with myself.

"He's no longer with us," the operator told me.

I replaced the receiver in its cradle and, like my former agent Rick Alan, emptied my desk of its clips, brads, staples, and chewed-up pencil stubs, slung my moosehead coatrack over my shoulder, went down to my rusty VW, climbed aboard, and drove out through the studio gate, managing to offer Scotty a final good-buddy smile.

And in all that time I'd never once seen Paul Newman.

Leaving Scotty and the Black Tower and C Building and Paul Newman's parking space behind, that day I chose the leisurely, scenic route home through a still-charred but reviving Griffith Park. Passing Travel Town and its restored historical railroad cars, I switched on the radio. It crackled to life with KRLA. "Fool on the Hill," from the lads' timeless and underappreciated *Magical Mystery Tour,* was mid-tune. Paul's angelic voice sang: "And the eyes in his head see the world spinning 'round."

31

TRULY LOST, I SOUGHT direction. Hollywood's rage du jour happened to be astrology. Major studio executives, and even government officials, were having their astral charts read, whatever that means, consulting with wizards and witches before making major corporate and political decisions. There was one crazy old hag in Venice, a certain Madame Blavatsky, who was said somehow to have acquired the power virtually to green-light pictures. Production chief Andy Albeck of United Artists would ultimately attempt to assign her the blame for *Heaven's Gate*. (He would lose his job all the same.)

In desperation, one bright Sunday I went to the Venice boardwalk, where Madame, astrologer to the stars, held court in her city-licensed tent. The perpetual love-in that throughout the sixties and much of the seventies had been Venice, California, was already devolving into a convention for panhandlers, drug addicts, and deranged, narcissistic outpatients.

I picked my way through the sea of weirdos and winos, past sword-swallowers, fire-eaters, chain-saw jugglers, and dope paraphernalia retailers. Bongs and coke spoons were in ample supply. There were so many roach clips available for purchase that the items were heavily discounted. For the most part they consisted of ratty pigeon feathers affixed to electrical alligator clips. One merchant gave them out free with the purchase of any water pipe. Another was so overstocked he actually paid a buck to anybody who would just take one away.

I joined the line at the entrance to the tent, where I spotted no small number of showbiz personalities, including executives Mike Marcus, Mike Levy, Mike Medavoy, Mike Hertzberg, and Mike Ovitz. And those were just the Mikes.

For over three hours I was hustled in at least eleven languages for spare change by no fewer than forty freaks. At last I was admitted to the tent's interior, where I was hustled once again, but for much more than spare change. Madame was the only hustler on the walk who took credit cards.

She also took some preliminary information: name, date of birth, height, weight, social security number, blood type, insurance carrier. She could have gotten the data from my driver's license. Then she drew a circle on a piece of paper and filled it with all sorts of arrows.

"Where are you?" she asked.

"I'm right here," I told her. The tent was dark and I imagined she had poor vision.

"That's not what I mean," she said. "Why are you here?"

"I need to answer certain questions about my life."

"Such as?"

"Where am I going? What am I doing? What should I do about my career? What should I do about my marriage?"

She nodded and shuffled a deck of cards, then laid none of them on the table. She took a rag from a tattered sack and polished up an actual crystal ball and then put it aside, never peering into it.

At last, she addressed me. "I need to look at Uranus," she said.

"I beg your pardon?" I wondered: Is this astrology or proctology?

She pored over papers that contained the names of the planets plus endless statistics. "The Earth," she said, studying her notes, "is poised just now between Saturn and Pittsburgh," she told me. And then she added, "This is highly unusual."

I didn't doubt it.

"The equally pulling stresses excite and energize the cosmos," she continued. "The polarity represents the requirement for balance among outer and inner constructs. You can be more aware of your societal agenda and your emotional initiatives. You need to find a creative way to share your personal vision with the world," she told me. "At the New Moon, the cycle is ready to replicate its original resonance. Does that clear things up for you?"

"Yes," I said. And then I said, "No, actually."

"Why, it's plain as day," Madame told me. "Here is the answer to all your questions, all your problems, your dissatisfactions, your disappointments. It's so simple. It's so obvious what you need to do. There is one, easy task for you to accomplish, and you will live in eternal bliss thereafter."

"What?" I asked, anxiously. "What task?"

"I'm afraid we have to stop now," she said, checking her watch. "That's all the time we have for today." Before I knew what was happening, she was ushering me out of the tent. CMA agent Mike Wise was just joining the line as I departed, and we exchanged courteous nods.

32

the MASSIVE SIGN I'D ordered—COMMERCIAL SUITES FOR RENT AND LEASE—clearly visible to cars rounding the freeway's cloverleaf, was just slightly smudged on one corner, and I paused to touch it up using a couple of bottles of Wite-Out. Then I hauled some empty cartons upstairs.

The door to what had been my downtown office was partially open, and I strolled in as casually as I could, all the while struggling to avoid peering at the shapely, nude young Asian woman perched perfectly still on the barstool in the middle of the floor. I tiptoed to the far corner where the last remnants of my gear stood in a shallow pile surrounding my moosehead coatrack.

I loaded the last of my scattered paraphernalia into the boxes, taking my time, all the while stealing surreptitious glances at the model's perfect almond-butter body. Her sculptor, my tenant, stood a hefty distance across the floor from her, before a mass of clay he was just now coaxing into a fair approximation of that stunning torso's pert and perky, rudely upturned left breast.

Soon enough, I was wholly moved out of the same warehouse, which I also wholly owned. I'd bought it super cheap—in those days real estate was given away free with an oil change—using the money I'd made in my now-aborted deal at Universal.

I rented the lofts to sculptors and painters. The spaces, many of them vacant for years, were all quickly snapped up, and the venture became obscenely profitable. But it was nothing compared to what would come in the downtown square-footage feeding frenzy that would soon be hard upon us.

And at the same time as I departed both Universal and my downtown quarters, Veronica and I and our daughters abandoned our Echo Park bungalow, but not before purchasing it, too, as income property. Veronica was earning something of a reputation as a second-unit director of sex scenes. Just as in the old days they would often bring in a specialist to shoot the fights, the battles, the car chases, they would hire Veronica to shoot the humping. These quick-and-dirty assignments paid a pretty penny and we were able to move into a spacious, rambling house in Pacific Palisades that was nearly as nice as the one we'd shared quite some years ago with Slade, Perry, and Troy when we were film students.

I took over the Pacific Palisades guest cottage—all by itself, it was larger than our entire Echo Park place—for my study. It was nestled at the property's edge amid shrubbery and gardens, past the magnificent used-brick patio and dark-blue-bottomed grottoesque waterfall-fed pool.

It seemed to me that at long, long last I was truly in California.

For the most part I spent my days performing hurry-up script-doctor chores, patching and polishing screenplays by other writers. For this, I was well paid but received no screen credit.

When we were all settled in, we threw a huge housewarming.

White-gloved red-jacketed valets met arriving guests at the end of the lengthy, meandering driveway. Inside the house and throughout the grounds, waiters and waitresses circulated with trays of drinks and hors d'oeuvres: flavorless Nouvelle curlicue cucumber things on whole-rye chips the size of Melba toast, smeared with lite this and organic that. I tasted one myself and discreetly spat it out into my cocktail napkin.

Veronica and I and our girls, Raynebeaux and Pacifica, stood in the entryway greeting the folks. Everyone from my entire West Coast life was present: Slade, Perry, Troy, and dozens of old film school pals. Perry seemed particularly frail; he couldn't have weighed a hundred pounds. And Troy's face was plastered with strategically placed mini–Band Aids. Also present were USC department chairman Kevin Burns, my old writing mentor, Professor Gordon Michaels, and virtually all the rest of the faculty. Even Zonker and his Hell's Angels buddies who'd appeared in *Brutal Bad-ass Angels* were present. Were they well behaved? As it turned out, the Hell's Angels were the best behaved of all our guests.

Adjunct Professor Jerry Lewis appeared. He seized Veronica at the door, wrapped his arms around her, mashed his face against her own, and jammed his tongue down to her tonsils. He kibitzed with my girls and pumped my hand relentlessly.

"She's some kind of piece of ass," he said. "Look at them buns! How 'bout them buns? Does she let you bang her from behind? Does she? Does she?" He turned to Veronica. "Do you let him bump your butt? You can tell me, honey. You can tell me. This is family talking here. You know what me and my wife like to do? We have one thing we like to do. Me and Patti, see, we go into the kitchen and she puts one knee, just one knee, understand, not two knees, just one knee up on the counter, right between the Cuisinart and the Crockpot, just beyond the fondue set, and I come around from the side, and then she . . . But that's another story."

He turned back to me. "You've really made it, Stu, buddy," he asserted. "You've really passed the Hollywood status test. And what's that? You think it's this fancy-ass ocean view house? Forget it. You think it's the wife with choice cheeks? Cheeks is bullshit by Hollywood, trust me. You think it's screen credits or fancy cars or Quaaludes and cocaine? Never mind, that ain't it. You know what it is? Do you? You know what's the authentic, genuine, bona fide, authorized, approved measure of Hollywood status? It's none of those things. None of them. Do you know what it is? Do you?"

"What is it?" I asked him.

"Valet parking."

At poolside people viewed haphazard jumpy old student films projected against the side of the guest house, very much in the fashion of the "screenings" back at our student pad when we were all tenants of Caltrans. People guzzled champagne and strawberries; they snorted tequila, and other substances as well.

Viewing the films, his head awash with nostalgia, Slade Sloan said, "Back then, these films all seemed so shabby. Now, given the years, they seem . . ." He paused long and hard, searching for precisely the proper characterization.

"Shabby?" Troy suggested.

"Exactly!" Slade agreed.

"They're certainly inventive, these films," opined Carter Elliott, the now-emeritus professor of film theory and criticism, "even if they never exactly worked as films."

"I kinda liked that movie," John Davilla, the production teacher said, on cue.

"A waveform monitor and shutter angle adjustment," slurred Pete Jenner, the ex–camera instructor, who was by now all too well into his cups, "would have eliminated the video strobe."

"It's zo, zo, zo—how shall we zay?—*américain!*" Chairman Kevin Burns announced in his funny phony French drawl.

"These pictures," screenwriting prof Gordon Michaels said, "remind me of films I worked on—under a nom de plume, naturally—during the blacklist years."

"Christ!" Burns said, returning to his regular voice. "You're not starting in on that blacklist horseshit again, are you?"

"It might be horseshit to a red-baiting turncoat like yourself, but to lots of people it was serious business," Michaels responded, nodding sagely, removing a tiny white nitro pill from a mosaic-tile-topped pillbox in his vest pocket and popping it under his tongue.

"Red-baiting turncoat?" Burns inquired, wide-eyed. "Are you talking about me or yourself?"

"Myself?" Michaels said, all innocent. "I'm the one who faced the committee in '53 and told them where they could stuff their damned inquisition."

"And what about your secret closed-session testimony three years later?" Burns asked, thrusting his chin high in the air, performing a fair impression of Il Duce.

Michaels was speechless. He dropped another nitro. "How'd you find out about that?" he stammered at last. "That was nothing. Purely pro forma, a petty procedural matter, no more. I'd been out of work for years. I was working in my brother-in-law's mother-fucking fluff-and-fold, for Christ's sake. I'd had my third, fourth, and fifth heart attacks by then. I told them nothing they didn't already know. I named no name that hadn't already been named on nameless, numerous, numberless occasions."

Michaels seemed sincerely rattled. He reached into his coat pocket and withdrew his hanky, too vigorously mopping his brow. Chairman Burns seemed somehow sorry that he'd said what he'd said. For a long moment, in what was otherwise a rollicking nonstop Hollywood gabfest, there was an awkward, painful silence. "Hey, Gordy," Burns said at last, "lighten up. Those were difficult days.

Lots of solid souls cracked just a little under the strain. You were merely human."

"They promised complete confidentiality," Professor Michaels said to nobody in particular, perhaps only to himself. He looked up at Burns. "Nobody was supposed to know about any of that. It was done in executive session. Who told you? Who told you about it? How'd you find out?"

"Are you kidding?" Burns asked, incredulous. "You trusted those witch-hunters to respect confidences? Everybody knows about it. Everybody."

"Who? Who told you?" Michaels insisted. "I'm curious."

Burns looked at him. "You want me to name names?"

Michaels reached forward and seized Burns's collar. "Don't fuck around with me, Kevin."

"I am not now, nor have I ever been, a stool pigeon," the chairman said.

"I warned you," Michaels told him. Shorter and fatter, he lunged at Burns, knocking him into the pool, where he immediately joined him, perhaps by accident, perhaps by design, attempting either to strangle him or cling to him to prevent his own drowning.

In another instant various people joined the fray. Perhaps they were trying to break it up; instead, they became very much a part of it. Soon the pool was filled with guests, for the most part fully clothed. The water foamed and frothed and chopped in the sweet and bitter brawl.

In a most curious way, the real-life party scene splendidly replicated the flashing intercut underwater images from the vintage student production *Extra Hot Sauce* just now unfolding on the guest cottage wall beside the pool.

33

the Falling-out between Professor Gordon
Michaels and Chairman Burns resulted in the former bolting USC
film school for crosstown rival UCLA.

In Westwood, Michaels routinely invited guest speakers to his
classes, but he eschewed superstar scribes, as they generally did only
two things: tell war stories and scan the skirts. He preferred, instead,
to invite what he called regular working writers, what others called
hacks, as these represented more realistic role models; they actually
discussed writing instead of bitching and carping about how they'd
been slighted by this producer on this project and snubbed by that
actor on that one.

"Don't put down hacks," he cautioned students repeatedly.
"You'll be goddamned lucky even to be a hack. Shakespeare was a
hack. If ol' Willie were around today, he'd be writing television. It'd
be the goddamned best television in history, of course, because the
guy happened to be a mother-jumping, jive-bombing genius. Remember," he asserted, "in this business it's a privilege even to be
mistreated. The worst thing of all is to be ignored. The worst thing
you'll hear in this town is nothing at all."

Perhaps it was this predilection for hacks that inspired him one day to invite me to perform a guest shot in his class; or perhaps a more highly esteemed guest had canceled at the last minute. In either case, I negotiated parking on the Westwood campus—hands down the major challenge in higher learning—and made my way to the Department of Film and Television by asking directions of at least forty people, some several of whom even spoke English.

To a recent 'SC cinema grad like myself, Westwood was the Promised Land. Instead of a ramshackle collection of hovels and huts, here was a sprawling, gleaming new plant replete with fully professional soundstages, a seventy-two-track dub-down theater, color video studios, a generous bank of state-of-the-art editing rooms with KEM flatbeds like the one my pals and I had purloined not too many years earlier. Of course, in so technical an enterprise as film, the state of the art changes every twenty minutes. What's brand-new today is antique tomorrow; what's unpacked fresh from the shipping crates on Tuesday stands curbside awaiting the trash collector Thursday.

As I approached the back entrance to Melnitz Hall I noticed red beacons flashing. As at any movie studio, these represent a plea that pedestrians tread lightly since, somewhere within, cameras are rolling.

And in the broad concrete courtyard outside the building there flashed now yet another red light; this one was mounted atop the roof of an ambulance. As I passed, paramedics sprang from the vehicle and sprinted before me into the building.

I made my way to the assigned classroom only to catch up with the paramedics, who were now exiting that same chamber. They carried a stretcher upon which lay Professor Gordon Michaels himself, white as a sheet, tubes in his nostrils, catheters in his veins. "Wait!" he gasped at the paramedics when he saw me. The white-suited men looked at him as if a strap needed adjustment. "I just want to talk to the guy for a minute," Michaels pleaded.

The paramedics hesitated.

"Never mind," I said to my old teacher. "Don't talk. Rest." I turned to the paramedics. "Go! Hurry!"

"Wait!" Michaels growled. "A little indisposed, is all," he gasped, as if to apologize. "Another little infarction, is all. I'm used to it already. A couple dozen more of these suckers and I'm outa here," he tried to joke. But agony and terror were evident in his grimace. "Stuart, listen," he importuned, "take over the class for today."

Take over the class? How in the world would I fill the time? I was slotted for a twenty-minute Q&A session. How would I fill three hours? "What do I do? What do I say?"

"You're a writer," Michaels told me. "Make it up as you go along."

The paramedics whisked Michaels away and I turned to regard a sea of faces belonging to students, all grouped around the doorway. I took a gulp of air and entered the seminar-sized classroom.

34

the students retreated from the doorway, returning to their seats around the table. I joined them, taking my place where Professor Gordon Michaels had sat only moments earlier. They looked at me expectantly, and I admit I was frightened.

What was to fear? I'd been surrounded by advantaged, privileged, competitive graduate students on countless occasions in recent and not-so-recent times. The difference was, of course, that now I was the goddamned instructor.

I found myself recalling my own very first day as a student, 1950, P.S. 11, Sunnyside, Queens. I decided to do what I always do when I'm scared: go for a laugh.

"Before we get started," I announced at last, as my teacher, Miss Howe, had announced back then, "I need to appoint a coatroom monitor." I scanned the group, expecting a laugh, or even merely a chuckle, or at the very least a smile. Surely I was entitled to a smile. But the students all sat there staring at me, dead serious. After a moment I added, "One-half letter-grade extra credit for the coatroom monitor. Do I have a volunteer?"

The students' hands rose en masse.

"There's no coatroom, for God's sake. This is California. There are no coats." After a moment I explained further, "It was a joke. Do you understand? A joke. Does everybody know what a joke is? Jokes, humor, these are among the many techniques that can be utilized even by screenwriters as they ply their trade."

The students seemed confused, but they put down their hands.

"Professor Michaels had intended this to be something of a question-and-answer session." I panned the room with my eyes, inviting inquiry.

"Does spelling count?" a student asked.

"Does counting spell?" quipped another. I was relieved to hear something resembling a gag. The ice was broken and now questions rained down fast and furious upon me.

"How do you get an agent?"

"Do you type your first draft or work in longhand?"

"If you type, do you use electric or manual?"

"If you work in longhand, do you use pencil or pen?"

"Or crayon?"

"Or felt-tipped marker?"

"If you work in longhand and by pencil, do you sharpen electric or manual?"

"How do you get an agent?"

"Do you use ruled yellow legal pads or blank white sheets?"

"Do you negotiate ancillary considerations—novelizations, spinoffs, coffee mugs, toys, and accessories—simultaneous to copyright?"

"How do you get an agent?"

The questions, frankly, appalled me. "These questions," I said, "frankly, appall me."

I stared back at the faces that stared back at me now in silence.

"Isn't anybody interested in the spiritual, emotional, intellectual aspects of writing? Are there no questions on character, story, dialogue, scene structure, language?"

The group appeared properly and appropriately chastened. I was overcome with the sweet expectation that perhaps I had served them well, had challenged them to confront their presumptions, provoked them into examining and exploring and evaluating heretofore uncritically embraced precepts. This teaching dodge might not be so bad, I thought, marinating in self-satisfaction.

After a hefty moment, at last a student's hand rose slowly, hesitantly.

I nodded in recognition.

"Two questions," he said, thoughtfully.

"Certainly," I chirped.

"First, is a writer better off," the student asked, "with an attorney who's also a packager, or should he maintain separate representation in those areas? And second—"

I cut him off, anticipating his next inquiry. "How do you get an agent?"

"Right." He nodded.

I sighed in defeat and despair.

35

PROFESSOR GORDON MICHAELS SURVIVED
his latest coronary, but he required a lengthy recuperation, and upon
his recommendation UCLA asked me to fill in for the rest of the
semester. Never mind that I found myself suddenly with an office—
an office without a phone, but an office; more impressive was my
Blue Permit, entitling me to a space in Parking Structure Three.

Even Paul Newman could not park in Structure Three.

I decorated my walls with our kids' finger paintings and a photo
of their mom standing between Ally Sheedy and Elizabeth McGov-
ern, who had co-starred in a moderately-budgeted film she had recently directed. The only item besides the university-issue desk and
chair and filing cabinet was a funky Indian cotton couch I'd picked
up cheap at a garage sale.

A department secretary appeared one day in the corridor outside
my new office and replaced the instructor's door card that read
"Gordon Michaels, Professor," with one reading "Stuart Thomas,
Acting In-Residence Adjunct Visiting Assistant Lecturer." It was
merely a temporary appointment, but somewhere in the back of my
head I was aware that fifteen full years had passed since I'd come
"temporarily" to California.

Lord knows there were worse places to while away one's days than the UCLA campus. The anger and turmoil characterizing the sixties were replaced not so much by serenity as somnambulism. Radical politics gave way to silence and a handful of fringe causes.

About the only truly active group was the gays.

Otherwise, all one ever saw was an occasional ecological ripple—for example, students carrying signs reading SAVE THE SNAIL DARTER. Here and there, religious fundamentalism had also established a toehold; there were posters along Bruin Walk reading JEWS FOR JESUS.

One fusion group even came up with banners proclaiming JEWS FOR THE SNAIL DARTER.

The film school bordered the sculpture garden, a world-class collection of eclectic excellence with pieces by the likes of Calder, Lipschitz, Rodin, and Moore, all elegantly, seductively scattered through lushly landscaped acres canopied by a riot of jacarandas that went hog-wild with lavender blossoms in the spring. In bloom, the garden could pass for a leftover sixties mescaline flashback.

I used to drag my ruled legal yellow pad to the sculpted green knolls and hollows to sketch out my continuing writing assignments, which happened still largely to consist of various script-doctor chores and other literary laundry: instructional, educational, motivational, informational, and commercial films, that is to say, corporate propaganda. The garden was the ideal place to work, except for the distractions—not the great and brilliant artworks but the leggy, statuesque California beauties in short shorts and skimpy no-bra halters.

There was life on the campus. People actually strolled; they did not drive, but walked from one place to another. This may not sound like all that much, but for Southern California it was really something. Campus offered the best of New York—a profusion of diverse human lives and textures and flavors and accents—minus the muggers and garbage and rotten weather.

There were fabulous first-rate eateries with inexpensive fresh food and cozy fires beside which to cuddle with a book during those few scattered days each year that passed for winter, when temperatures would plunge into the fifties. God's true purpose, no doubt, in providing such days, was merely to provide a field against which to appreciate the otherwise perpetual balmy breezes and fresh sea air and sunshine. Smog? Here on the west side, a scant mile from the ocean, purported pollution was but a scam devised to discourage still more New Yorkers from relocating.

As if all that weren't enough, I had now at my disposal the best research facilities: no fewer than eighteen libraries, bunches of museums and galleries right on campus, plus the largest television archive in the world, to say nothing of the film collection, which was second only to that of the Library of Congress.

It was a mighty handy place for a writer.

And not the sculpture garden alone but the entire campus was aswarm with women. Though I was very much a married fellow whose bride was fit and fair as ever, I became aware also that a married man is not a dead man. After all, just because you're on a diet doesn't mean you can't look at the menu.

Given the bounty of resources and attractions, it was inevitable that I would spend less time at my guest-cottage office at home and more on campus. Home was too damned peaceful, too convenient. With my daughters in school and in day care, nobody ever disturbed me. And every writer, no matter how he protests to the contrary, lives for disruption. On campus, not only were there students to burst in upon me and ask me questions and chat and gossip and schmooze, but also departmental support staff, photocopying services personnel, folks to greet, folks to whom one could say: "Hi, hello, nice to see you, how you doing?"

It may not sound like much, but for isolated, moody, cranky, cantankerous writers it is a big deal indeed.

I knew I had relocated onto the campus for good the day I moved to my office the musky, molting moosehead coatrack.

36

i loved my new campus life so well that from time to time it scared me just a bit; I worried I would end up like my colleague and Macgowan Hall next-door neighbor, crazy old professor Ted Bradshaw.

One night I had been working particularly late in the office on perhaps the most singularly tedious writing assignment since writing itself was invented in ancient Sumeria or Babylonia or wherever it was, six thousand years ago: a trade show for a toy company.

Why had I accepted such an assignment? Veronica was working steadily for the major studios now, and for increasingly steep fees. Still, in Hollywood it's feast or famine, and I simply could not shake the habit of working on whatever was offered.

Certainly our household enjoyed a comfortable income. Nevertheless, expenses were also mounting. I half expected Veronica would urge me to reject such assignments as the toyfest. Wouldn't it stifle my creativity? Shouldn't I follow my heart? Shouldn't I create my own unique voice, tell my own personal story, construct my particular perspective on the human condition?

I expected Veronica would reprimand me for taking assignments such as this deadening toy show. To the contrary, she asserted that it was solid drill, a chance for an artist to polish his skills, to hone his craft. Whenever she used the "A" word, whenever she called me an artist, I was helpless. Additionally, she noted that even if we had already saved up enough money to send our daughters to college, we were spending it all on their upscale elementary school education.

As always, I did whatever Veronica told me. Did I resent her for her control? Or was I grateful? Was it her power over me that I found so alluring, so seductive, so attractive?

Socrates said that true wisdom is knowing that you do not know. By this standard I was wise indeed.

For the toy company, I was charged with smearing wall-to-wall narration across what was really nothing more than a two-hour slide show depicting next year's line. The job was every bit as lucrative as it was boring, and I did not especially object to working late that particular night, and not only because the pay was good. I appreciated also that upon handing in the pages the next morning I would have this uniquely onerous opus forever behind me.

I had just written what must surely be my most timeless line: "Tammel takes an aggressive stance in the Large Doll area." Large Dolls, apparently, was one of several product categories. My favorite sounded like a double bill in San Francisco's Castro district: "Boys' Toys and Male Action Figures."

I knew for certain that if I did not take a break I would quite simply and without fanfare hang myself from the harsh fluorescent fixture lighting my office. A nighttime stroll through the sculpture garden was just the ticket.

I arose from my desk and plunged into the corridor—it must have been three-thirty in the morning—to discover Bradshaw's door wide open. This in and of itself was an exceedingly rare event; Bradshaw's chamber was otherwise perpetually sealed, like a vault. No student, no staff member, no faculty colleague had ever been inside.

Even the janitors could not get in to clean, as Bradshaw had changed the lock. Technically this represented a violation of fire regulations, but nobody, not even the pettiest power-crazed bureaucrat, dared cross Bradshaw, who was clinically mad. Rumor had it that years earlier he'd logged time in stir, for nobody knew quite what.

Of course, I could not resist a peek within. Jammed into the impossibly cramped quarters were a made-up bed, a hot plate, and an old-fashioned armoire. I turned and started down the hall toward the stairway, when I suddenly caught sight of Ted himself exiting the men's room. He was dressed in pajamas and a robe. He carried a toothbrush. A worn terry towel was thrown across his shoulder.

Clearly, Macgowan Hall was the old dude's residence! When he was finally forced to retire years later, for some while he relocated to a storage closet in the basement.

Eventually, ill health required Professor Michaels to retire, and I inherited his appointment. At my own expense, I fixed up the office into commodious, congenial quarters, laying in a parquet floor, cedar-paneling the walls, and adding a host of homey, personal touches designed, along with the moosehead coatrack, to render the chamber an agreeable workspace.

One mid-morning, while I punched up some bureaucratic curricular proposal, there was a knock at my door. A student, Warren Robbins, appeared. Robbins was most notable for how unnotable he was; in a sea of wildly creative individuals, here was someone who was especially unspecial.

"Do you have my script?" he inquired.

I reached into the pile of assignments, seized his, and handed it to him. He peered hard at the back cover. "B?" he said. "You call that a fair grade? You really believe I deserve a B?"

"No, actually."

"Then how do you justify it?"

"Even if it's not quite worth a B," I responded, "the grade reflects my belief that it can be brought up to that level with a vigorous rewrite."

"Wait a minute," Robbins protested. "Writing just happens to be something I know a little bit about."

"I quite agree," I could not resist saying.

"You simply can't relate to the theme," the student insisted. "That's the problem right there. You can't tolerate the story of a young homosexual's coming of age without his being depicted as perverse."

"Not at all," I said. "I'm merely encouraging you to pay closer attention to language and craft."

"You're punishing me for being a faggot, is what you're doing," he said, with a flat affect.

"Nonsense," I said. "Your sexuality is your own business."

"I won't sit here and be judged by you," Robbins asserted.

"Respectfully," I said, "I have a covenant with the Regents requiring me to do just that, to judge you in so far as your performance in this class is concerned. My judgment consists of that letter grade and, frankly, B is pretty damned good."

"This script is A work. A-plus. It's going to win the Mayer Screenwriting Competition. I'll lose my assistantship with a B. I'll be kicked out of school. It'll kill my mother. She's got colitis."

I'd been at the job only a short while, but had already heard my fair share of sob stories. "How do you figure a B will cause you to be kicked out of school?" I asked.

"You sit there"—he breathed deeply—"crippled by your own narrow straightness, rendering bigoted judgments on imaginative, innovative artists like me because we adopt an unorthodox lifestyle that threatens your complacency and your slavish devotion to the straight, white, Western Euro-centered industrial male canon," he said calmly. After a moment he continued, "I'm going to give you one last chance to be reasonable. Will you change my grade?"

"Truly, Warren," I said, feeling sorry for the fellow, sincerely trying to reach him, "you're making entirely too much of this. It's merely a grade."

Warren Robbins stared at me. He continued staring at me for a good moment. He said at last, too quietly, "Will you or will you not change this grade?" He posed it as an interrogatory, but it bore the cadence of a declaration.

"You ask me a direct question," I said. "You're entitled to a direct answer: No."

He shrugged, rolled his eyes casually back into his forehead, and began to unbuckle his jeans. "What in the world are you doing?" I asked him.

He pulled his pants and shorts down to his knees. "Help! Help!" he screamed.

"What's the matter?" I inquired urgently. "What are you doing?"

Robbins now ripped open his shirt, rending the fabric, sending the buttons flying like shrapnel. "Please! Somebody!" he screamed. I watched in terror and crazy awe as he now messed up his own hair and scattered scripts and papers all about the office. In another moment he turned over several items of furniture, including an oaken two-drawer file cabinet and my moosehead coatrack.

"What in the world are you doing?" I asked yet again.

"Let me go!" he yelled. "Please, Professor! Please! I can't! Don't!

No! Don't!" And now he bolted for the door, seized the knob, turned it, yanked the door open, and charged out into the corridor.

I followed him out into the hall, where the commotion had already attracted just a little bit of a mob. I looked at a panorama of faces belonging to colleagues and students and now spotted the department chairman himself making his way down the hall. They all stared second at me but first at the student Warren Robbins, shirt-tails flapping, balls flopping, stumbling crazily along the corridor in apparent flight.

"Help!" Robbins cried to all who were assembled. "Rape! Don't let him near me! Please! He tried to rape me!"

And now a campus cop appeared. "What's going on here?" the officer demanded, trying to catch his breath.

Darkness sank upon me as everyone stared. "It's not the way it looks," I stammered. "I swear! He suddenly started shouting and . . ." I ran out of steam as I peered into the faces regarding me with shock, suspicion, and disgust. I looked down the long tunnel of my future and saw nothing but dishonor and revulsion heaped upon me. I imagined faculty committee hearings and investigations, deans' resolutions of reprimand and censure, and costly litigation. Just as I had begun to accept the job as an agreeable lifetime arrangement, it was sabotaged.

At this precise moment my neighbor, Professor Ted Bradshaw, opened his own rarely opened office door and stepped out into the corridor wearing the same ratty brown brushed-wool robe I'd seen that one other occasion so late at night months earlier. "Officer?" Bradshaw said quite calmly. "May I say something?"

All eyes now turned to Ted.

The walls in our faculty offices were paper thin. Bradshaw, cooking up a gourmet onion-and-bell-pepper omelet on his hot plate, had overheard the entire exchange between me and Warren Robbins. Within minutes he had exposed the student's grim little scam for what it truly was and, in doing so, of course, also saved my Acting In-Residence Adjunct Visiting Assistant professorial butt, my academic career.

37

beFORe i COULD QUite turn around, several years flew
by and suddenly I found myself yet again outside my office door at
the beginning of yet another academic year, this time in the company of my positively gorgeous, maturing daughters, Raynebeaux
and Pacifica, and their positively gorgeous, maturing mother, Veronica, who held in her hands a bottle of hundred-dollar champagne.
We watched as a department secretary replaced my "Instructor"
door card with one reading simply "Stuart Thomas, Professor."

I had won what is perhaps the last, best thing in Western civili-
zation: tenure.

Veronica popped the cork, and in clear contravention of well-
established university norms and procedures, we consumed just a
smidgen of alcohol—yes, even the girls took a nose-wrinkling cer-
emonial sip—right there on the campus. And from there we went
directly down the stairs and over to the next building, the Melnitz
Theater.

The broad brick-and-glass-and-concrete facade of Melnitz was
festooned with a banner proclaiming: WOMEN FILMMAKERS—A VE-
RONICA BALDWIN RETROSPECTIVE. I, my wife, and our daughters—
a handsome, happy group—made our way past lines of Veronica's

fawning, adoring fans. Who could believe she'd already garnered sufficient credits and celebrity to warrant her own retrospective?

Inside the darkened hall, the tail credits to *Brutal Bad-ass Angels* concluded, the house lights came up, and there was a standing, stamping, stomping, stampeding ovation. Student hopefuls rushed forward, mobbing me and Veronica and the girls. As wanna-bes surged around us, thrusting programs at Veronica, seeking her autograph, hurling questions and praises galore, I actually became fearful for my children's safety and led them away a short distance beyond the knot in the crowd.

As we waited patiently for the storm of adulation to subside, an exceptionally fresh, sparkling eighteen-year-old, a girl-woman with hazel eyes who seemed at once savvy and naive, made her way up to me. While she was a total stranger, she seemed uncannily familiar. "Thanks for the advice," she said to me.

I turned this way and that. Finally I said, in a fair approximation of Travis Bickle, "You talking to me?"

"Yes," she said, looking me directly in the eye.

"Advice?" I asked her.

"Yes," she said again. "I've enrolled."

"Enrolled?" I asked.

"In film school," she said. "I've enrolled in film school, exactly as you recommended." After a moment she peered down at her feet, clearly disappointed. "You don't remember me."

"Of course I do," I lied.

"Bull," she said. "A few years ago I sort of hanged myself on the back lot at Universal and you sort of saved me."

"Sure!" I said, remembering clearly and completely. "You had a mouthful of metal."

"And a face full of pimples," Ginger Kenton said, brightening. "I was barely menstruating then," she volunteered in a let-it-all-hang-out, do-your-own-thing, sixties, "sharing" sort of way.

"Yes," I said.

"I'm registering for your advanced screenwriting course this semester."

"You've taken the prerequisite introductory fundamentals lecture class and the concomitant preparatory seminar-workshop section?"

"Of course not. I just got here."

"You'll need those courses first," I explained, "plus the signed recommendation of your adviser, as well as the chairman, and also the consent of the instructor."

"You're the instructor," she said.

"That's true," I conceded, "but it doesn't mean I'm not bound by various constraints placed upon all faculty by the department, the division, the university, and the regents." No doubt it was my mastery of such jargon that had gotten me tenure in the first place.

"Listen up, Professor," Ginger Kenton said smoothly. "You gave me advice and the time has now arrived for me to return the favor. Ready?"

She paused briefly, allowing her sweet and cocky arrogance to sink in. "Don't let the administration fuck you over. They're a bunch of clerks, mindless bureaucrats, keypunch–punch clock kings and queens. They work for you, not the other way around, get it? You didn't arrive at your own high level of achievement, you did not accomplish all that you've accomplished, by letting petty procedures, meager rules and regulations, stand in the way of your creativity and authority as both an artist and educator."

I was surprised to find myself rather admiring her assertiveness. Self-assurance would not hurt anyone hoping to compete in mainstream Hollywood. But where does confidence end and disrespect begin? The power vested in me via my rank had made me expect people to kiss my ass just a little bit, instead of ordering me around.

"They'll waive all that crap if you'll only ask them," Ginger Kenton continued. "Myself, I've no time for it. I'm in a hurry to be a film artist, and I'm going to permit you to help."

I searched the files of my cortex for something, anything, to offer by way of a response, and as I did so the strange and strangely wonderful creature turned and dissolved into the crowd.

At last, several moments after she was gone, I said to nobody in particular, merely to the ether surrounding me, "I admire your pluck, of course, but I'm afraid it's truly out of the question."

38

EVEN AS I SAID it, even as I announced to thin air that under no circumstances would I admit Ginger Kenton to my advanced class, I knew I lied. I knew that, for absolutely no reason I could understand, I would permit her to do anything she pleased. I would permit her to use and abuse me, to exploit me, to wreck me and ruin me and break my sore and sorry heart.

What possessed me even to consider cooperating with the smug, scheming little creature? Was it something in me? Was it something in Ginger?

Was it both?

At the time, I had no earthly idea, and now, much later, after substantial contemplation and rumination, I have no earthly idea.

In an attempt to answer these painful questions, in an effort generally to address the gnawing disquietude within me, the self-deprecation that resided in my every cell, I sought help with a then widely ballyhooed self-help psychological support group. I told Veronica, who was always wary of Hollywood's pop therapies du jour, that I was going only to make showbiz contacts among the many executives who regularly participated in such events.

The event, an intensive and expensive meeting-lecture-seminar-workshop lasting an entire weekend, was held at the spanking new Los Angeles Convention Center downtown, where the marquee read: "AST—Assertiveness Sensitivity Training—A Final Solution to the Happiness Problem."

The vast hall was jammed. The ticket was as hard—$475 in early Ronald Reagan dollars—as the chairs, cold metal folding jobs proffering precious little by way of comfort. Indeed, discomfort was in many ways the weekend's organizing principle.

Counselors and auditors and facilitators, employees of the organization running the show, prowled the aisles like the Gestapo, here and there forming clusters in order to challenge and confront and provoke a particular soul trapped within. I say "trapped," because once everyone was inside the hall, the doors were sealed and locked—I don't doubt that doing so violated fire regulations—and nobody could leave, not for any purpose whatsoever.

All the auditors, call them oppressors, wore starched white shirts and slacks and gleaming white sneakers. Frankly, I clung to my sanity that weekend by imagining them also to be wearing those chrome-plated small-change-makers on their belts that the Good Humor ice cream vendors wore in my neighborhood back in Queens. I had to suppress an urge to request a toasted-coconut pop. For hours I sat there quietly, stupidly, and watched them attack this guy here and that guy there.

At long last came my turn.

"Because you're a limp-wristed pushover," one of the auditors shouted at me point-blank, scant inches from my face.

"A coward," his compatriot agreed.

"A wimp," the first guy said.

"A sucker," said yet another.

"You disgust me."

"You make me sick."

"You're revolting."

"Repellent."

"Retarded."

"Ree-diculous."

"And those are just the 'ree's."

"You're stomach-turning."

"Nauseating."

"You don't deserve to live, to breathe the same air as decent, upstanding, honorable, responsible people . . ."

". . . to occupy the same space as solid, deserving, achieving, worthy souls."

By now the various tormentors surrounding me had merged into one. When they paused for air, I managed politely to mumble, "I think I get your point, but at the same time I wonder if you're being entirely fair."

"You talk to us of 'fair'? If the world were fair you'd be dust. Your contemptible, loathsome, despicable bones would lie buried deep beneath us by now, if there were an ounce of justice on God's green earth. Your life has all the impact of a lamprey eel's, and you prattle on about being 'fair'?"

When the speaker ran out of breath, his pal took over. These guys were a regular therapy tag team. "A bobbing cork is all you are. You've got the purpose and direction and usefulness of a fresh, steaming lump of shit. Is that fair? Is it?"

"No, wait a minute," said another member of the team. Gesturing toward me, addressing his colleagues, he said, "He's right." I was momentarily surprised. I did not expect any of them to agree with me about anything. "It's not fair," he said again, nodding, "to compare you to a steaming lump of shit," he reiterated. "It's not fair to the steaming lump of shit."

"If you had even a fragment of one single testicle, you'd tell the skanky little slut to go straight to hell, Professor."

"I'm her teacher."

"She's your teacher."

"You should be your own goddamned teacher."

"You're her slave."

"You're everybody's slave."

"I owe her support."

"She owes you, jerk."

"Fool."

"Moron."

"Cretin."

"Retard."

"Asshole."

"Idiot."

"Enabler."

"Victim."

There was now a long pause, during which nobody said anything. At last, overwhelmed by pressure from my overfilled bladder, I moved to rise. "I'll think about all that," I assured them all, "and I'll be right back."

But they shoved me back into my chair.

"You're not going anywhere."

"I've got to go to the bathroom."

"You've got to take responsibility for your life and not pawn it off to every wretched little whim, every twerpy little creep who just happens to drift along in the maelstrom of emotional sewage that passes for your life."

"Today is the first day of the rest of all the bullshit."

"Are you never going to own yourself?"

"Stand up for yourself?"

"Will you never, not even once, address your own needs, your own merit—if there's a shred of merit in you?"

"Your wife fucks jungle bunnies and you raise the mongrel offspring as your own with nary a whimper of protest?"

"I really don't like that kind of talk one bit," I protested meekly. "I happen to abhor bigotry. A child is a child. I love the child."

"Your purported pals steal your movie credit, and you're Mr. Good Guy?"

"And your answer is to go pee-pee?"

"You pose and posture and strut as if you're something or somebody, but you're not. You're nobody. You're nothing. You wander through life's motions, but you're dead. You're a failed writer, a failed human. Failure is your success. Failing's the one thing you do to perfection. You're not merely a failure; you're a perfect failure."

I was appalled by this abuse, but was there not some substance to what I was being told? Were these hundreds of fellow seminarians all fools, or was there something useful to be derived from the weekend?

"And what in the world," I asked quite sincerely, at long last surrendering, "am I supposed to do about it?"

"I'm sorry," the leader said, checking his watch, directing the group toward its next victim, "but that's all the time we have for today."

39

WHATEVER INNER TURMOIL BESIEGED me, on the surface my nice, neat life dripped and drabbed along comfortably enough and I was motivated neither to complain nor to change. Life on campus was a sweet and constant distraction.

In good weather—we had virtually nothing but—I held class in the sculpture garden.

"I can't decide precisely which genre to attack," volunteered a student, joining the class late. We held a story session where we sat in a circle in the soft, cool grass in the shade of a two-piece Moore. "Dramatic comedy or comedy? Melodrama or drama? Action? Adventure? Mystery? Thriller? Character? Youth? Horror? Caper? Nostalgia? Romance?"

"There are only two genres," I told him. "Class?"

My dutiful parrots recited in unison: "Good movies and bad movies."

"I see," the student said halfheartedly, not really seeing at all. "And how do we tell the difference?"

"A good movie," I explained patiently, "merits the time, attention, and consideration of an audience. It merits also the three and a half bucks a ticket now costs in Westwood. A bad movie does not."

"I have another answer," Ginger Kenton announced, "the real, true answer." Although she had never bothered to take the prerequisite introductory course, without any hassle she was admitted to the advanced section, having succeeded in conning the instructor into awarding his consent. How had she accomplished this? How had she succeeded in bullying her newly assertive professor? By coming to class anyway; by insisting upon attending even if she was never signed in; by making it quite perfectly clear that campus security was the only way she would be removed; quite frankly, by, shaming the instructor into enrolling her.

I signed her Permission to Enroll slip the second week.

"Oh?" I said as casually as I could, a bogus devil-may-care Michael-Landon-furrowed-brow atop my all-patient, all-tolerant face. "And please tell us precisely what is the real, true answer."

"The real, true answer," Ginger Kenton said, "is that a good movie is one that your instructor likes, and a bad movie is one that he does not."

A lesser educator would have been put off by her curt, blunt arrogance, might even have viewed it as disrespect. I was myself, of course, above such limitations, fully able to appreciate creativity's need not merely to tolerate but to welcome, even eagerly to solicit challenge and provocation. There would be ample opportunity at the conclusion of the semester, in our individual tutorial meeting, calmly and properly to reassert my superior authority. The meeting was a central feature of my advanced class, set aside for the purpose of discussing each student's script.

Such meetings were held not in the sculpture garden but in my office. And that is where I sat several weeks later, alone with Ginger Kenton. She had dressed for the meeting: loose, fragile halter and super-short skirt exposing a frail excuse for panties—red lace bikini cut with a delicate spiderweb pattern woven into the crotch—that I was too, too serene even to notice.

" 'Alley Rats,' " I read, fingering her script, riffling through the hundred-plus misspelled, incorrectly punctuated, and otherwise ungrammatical pages. "Excellent title."

"Did you get any further than that?" she asked.

Beneath her glitzy tough-guy sheen I really rather liked the child. It struck me somehow that here might well be an artist worth supporting. "There are promising elements," I said.

"Elements," she repeated flatly. "Promising." She took a deep breath and let it out slowly. "You hate it."

"You don't want me to patronize you," I said. "It's a hodgepodge of disconnected images signifying nothing. Empty. Hollow. Pretentious. Silly."

"So you're on the fence about it," she quipped darkly. "You can't make up your mind one way or the other." For a moment she said nothing. Then she said, "Please don't worry about my feelings. Those among us who engage in creative expression have to learn to deal with criticism. I can take it. If you don't like the script, you may say so."

Was this light banter or a demonstration of her willingness to accept criticism? True artists, I had learned as a writer and writing educator, required both talent and stamina, but a lot of the latter and a little of the former took them further than the converse combination. The ability dispassionately to consider criticism was essential. I continued undeterred, "It appears to be little more than exploitation."

"Like *Brutal Bad-ass Angels?*" she said. "What's wrong with exploitation? It means 'making the most of,' right? What's so godawful about reaching people?"

"That's fine for Hollywood," I told her, "but here in the university we're free to venture beyond mere trade and trafficking. We're free to move beyond whatever it is the studios are buying this week. We're free from time to time even to fall flat on our faces. We're free to experiment."

"Thanks so much for that," she said, a trace of bitterness leaching into her tone. "But isn't all art, is not all creative expression experiment? Is not the lowliest *Charlie's Angels,* after all is said and done, merely an experiment? Is not the silliest, most superficial sketch on *Sonny and Cher* an experiment? Is not art in its nature first and foremost experiment?" She took a long pause to let all this sink in. I admit I was impressed by what she said and how she said it.

She added, "You taught me that."

"I did?"

Indeed, she had merely reiterated what had become my too-familiar party line.

"You urge me to study in film school," she pressed her case. "You twist my arm to take your course. At your insistence I devote time and energy—and no small amount of cash earned waitressing—precisely to study with you. Have you no sense of obligation?"

"Obligation?"

"To see to it that I get this script right." She squirmed in place, wiggling her butt where she sat, advancing one cheek at a time until she was poised at the edge of the couch. She leaned forward, causing the halter's top to fall open not a little bit, proffering an unfettered view of her breasts, the nipples so pebbly stiff and sharp they would surely slice the skin of the hand or lip that dared brush them. "You can help me make this script work," she whispered in a smoky rasp. "You can. I know you can."

She paused.

"I have confidence in you," she reassured me.

40

THE CAMPUS PULSED AND throbbed and swarmed with the cutest cuties in creation, the vast majority among them more alluring, more compelling, more responsible, more reasonable than Ginger Kenton. What was it, then, to account for my devotion to her? What could explain her power over me?

I knew the answer to the question and I did not doubt that it was the right answer, but I knew also that it was wholly unsatisfying. The answer was: I don't know.

But true scholars and artists seek not answers but, rather, increasingly refined questions.

The refined question in my life at that moment was: Why am I sitting here in my faculty office, surrounded by notepads and index cards, oblivious to time, day, and date, writing and re-rewriting a student's screenplay? The sun had come up and gone down and up and down several times. Here and there and now and again I had catnapped. Here and there I had scarfed down a candy bar or sucked up a stale, flat, too-sweet-syrupy vending-machine Coca-Cola Classic when it was still just Coke.

Of course it was inappropriate for me to do so, but relentlessly I trimmed and kneaded and shaved and snipped and sculpted and molded. Slowly the script improved. Gradually it took on shape and tale and thematic heft. I felt myself approaching something that resembled the perfect Aristotelian end, that point after which there is nothing.

There came a tentative knock at my door.

Veronica stood in the corridor. "Working late?" she asked.

Late? I had been missing from my own life for nearly a couple of weeks already. I had let her believe I was working on yet another commercial - industrial - instructional - educational - informational - corporate movie for a pharmaceutical company addressing therapies to treat bladder infections in preadolescent, adult, and postmenopausal women.

I squinted down at my watch; in my exhaustion, it took me a moment to interpret the digits. "It's too early to be late," I said. "It's already early again. You schlepped all the way to campus? You should have called."

Veronica gestured with her chin toward the phone which lay off the hook.

"I needed to work without interruption," I mumbled.

"I figured you had young pussy in here."

"I do," I said, looking at my wife. "Slide out of them panties right now."

"Panties?" she said. "What're panties? Who's wearing panties?" My partner of many years pulled up her skirt and flashed. The familiar smooth and prickly pale-caramel bush excited me as much as always. Exhausted as I was, I was not so weary as to be incapable of arousal. I gestured toward the couch and unhitched my pants, but Veronica stood her ground. "You forgot," she said.

"What did I forget? I forget what I forgot."

"*Home* magazine," she said. "The *L.A. Times* Sunday supplement."

" 'At Home With . . .' us?" I asked.

And now a photographer and reporter stepped from behind Veronica, where all the while they had lurked. "We can grab some snaps right here," the journalist instructed his photographer, gesturing around my office, "and then move on to the house, the children, the dogs and cats and fish and all that." He turned to Veronica. "Mrs. Thomas?" he said. "Wanna slide in there beside the ol' p'rfess'r?"

Veronica took up a position at my side, leaning against my desk. Movie director that she was, she was fully familiar with the fine points of configuring bodies.

The camera clicked and the strobe strobed.

Soon enough the entire operation was transported to our house. I, Veronica, and our daughters all got into swim gear and grouped ourselves in various poses around the pool. We changed wardrobe again and retired indoors to strut and posture before the fireplace.

The photographer's assistant turned on the gas jets and set the ceramic logs ablaze. "It's a hundred and nine degrees outside; who needs a roaring fire?" I protested.

"Like myself, Professor Thomas," the reporter explained, "you're a writer. We're Word People, you and I, aren't we? Photographers, on the other hand, are Image People. Take Mrs. Thomas. . . ."

"Please!" I could not resist saying. "Somebody! Anybody!"

"She understands the effect of visually enhanced graphic design methodology."

"He means," Veronica explained flatly, "the room shoots prettier with fire."

"Anybody got a marshmallow?" I asked with a straight face.

41

"NO, NO, NO, NO, no," Ginger Kenton said, looking down at the script on the table before us, shaking her head sternly, grimacing in disapproval. She leafed through pages of the screenplay, "Alley Rats," that I had rewritten.

She was a vision, to be certain, in her white flowing robes and Sikh turban. The Holistic Harmony Health and Healing Restaurant was tucked in a remote corner of a Westwood side street. I had already spent more than a decade on the campus but still couldn't get the names of the streets. Was it Glendon? Weyburn? Landfair? Kinross?

Whatever the street's name, it was virtually deserted at this odd midafternoon hour, too late for the lunch crowd and too early for dinner. "Wrong, wrong, wrong, wrong, wrong," she asserted, studying the pages still further.

"So you're on the fence about it," I said.

"You don't want me to patronize you," she explained.

"You can't make up your mind one way or the other," I said. "Please don't worry about my feelings," I assured her. "Those among us who engage in creative expression have to learn to deal with criticism. I can take it. If you don't like the script, you may say so."

"It's just not clicking," she said.

"It's your script," I told her bluntly. "Make it click."

"Oh, sure," she said. "I could choose the easy path. I could take it out of your hands entirely, quit school, work it out on my own." She peeked up at me from beneath those fluttering lashes. Her voice sank to a sweetly scratchy whisper. "You're my teacher," she said breathily. "My success or failure reflects upon you. My struggle is to make you look good. Don't you want to look good?"

"What I want," I complained, "is lunch."

Ginger turned on her heel and fled. I looked down at the table and perused several pages of the script. Was it any good? I admit I was confused.

She reappeared at my side. "Crystal Chrysanthemum Salad," she said, slamming hard upon the table a heavy ceramic bowl heaped high with greens. A handful of garbanzos rolled down onto the cloth, and two among them fell to the floor.

Another landed in my lap.

I seized it, tossed it in my mouth, and chewed.

Ginger stared at the salad. "You got sprouts, kale, escarole, sesame seeds, poppy oil, Port vinegar, and fresh mustard-and-organic-honey dressing."

"Delicious!" I said, swallowing the garbanzo.

"Yeah?" she said in disbelief. "Never catch me eating that crap. Choke to death on the motherfucking sprouts." She peered surreptitiously around the restaurant. Then she whipped a Big Mac from inside her robes and inhaled it.

"What about your holistic principles?" I asked her, gesturing toward the vanishing Mac.

"I'm a waitress here, period," she said, swallowing the burger. "I may have to wear this idiot costume, but I don't have to eat this dreck. If management knew I'd smuggled flesh into the joint—never mind that it's beef, a sacred cow—they'd throw me out on my fine, round ass."

"They'd fire you for that?"

"Fire me? These dear, sweet, gentle, celestial souls would pluck out my holistic pubic hairs one by one." She looked at the salad, which I had barely had time to touch. "You finished with that?"

"What's the hurry?"

"You've got to get back to work."

"The studios don't drive their writers so hard," I protested.

"I want to enter 'Alley Rats' in the Mayer Competition. We're up against a deadline."

"I ought to know something about the Mayer deadline," I told her. "I'm one of the judges."

I managed to grab a first real bite of the salad before she seized it from me and sprinted for the kitchen. "Write!" she called over her shoulder. "Write!"

And she disappeared through the swinging doors.

I sat there quite thoroughly alone except for the pages of "Alley Rats." After a moment I plucked a couple of remaining garbanzos from where they lay on the table. I tossed them into my mouth and chewed them ever so slowly.

42

IF MY MACGOWAN HALL neighbor, Professor Ted Bradshaw, objected to round-the-clock typing rattling through the flaky plasterboard separating our offices, he was certainly a good sport about it; he never said a word. I knew from the tantalizing aroma circulating through the building's air-conditioning ducts that he was presently frying up a delicate plate of turkey sausage and eggs. I could also smell dry, nutty fresh coffee brewing.

I paused in my rewriting—a fourth or fifth or sixth draft, I'd lost count—of Ginger Kenton's script and heard from the hallway a curious ratchet sound and now also a rhythmic squeaking. This was followed by a loud, rude thump in the hall as if an object of some heft had hit the floor.

Wearily I rose from my swivel chair, took the short few steps to the door, and opened it to find Ted's door opening, too. He bent to lift the oversized *Los Angeles Sunday Times* that had just been deposited at his doorstep. The newspaper delivery boy, riding a bike whose chain sorely needed grease, was just now disappearing down the far end of the hall.

Standing on the floor outside Bradshaw's door beside the paper was also a container of milk, a stick of butter, and a dozen eggs. Ted, in pajamas and slippers, nodded at me but did not smile and I felt a bit awkward, an intruder.

"Want a piece of the paper?" he asked, surprising and pleasing me.

Before I could respond he handed me some random sections. And before I could properly thank him he had already retreated to his lair and sealed the door.

"Thanks," I mumbled to the air in the corridor.

I repaired to my own warren, dumped myself in the swivel and dropped the newspaper in my lap. Staring back at me from the cover of *Home* magazine was a glowing portrait of me, Veronica, and the girls, all of us grouped cozily around the roaring fire in our living room in Pacific Palisades. The copy read: "Who Says You Can't Have It All? Happiness in Hollywood: At Home with Stuart and Veronica Baldwin Thomas—A Blissful, Loving Family Positively Drippy-Gooey with Serenity and Success."

The door swung open and there stood Bradshaw yet again, a steaming cup of coffee in his hand. "Use a cup?" he asked me.

"I would kill for a cup," I confessed.

He handed it to me. "Cream?"

"No thanks," I said.

"Milk?"

"Thanks," I told him, "no."

"I got four percent and two percent and no percent."

"Black's just right."

"I got nondairy whitener if you suffer from lactose allergies."

"Love it black," I said, drawing satisfyingly from the cup.

"Sugar? I got white and I got brown. Got granulated, got powdered. Got cubes. Got caramelized, got refined, got raw."

"None, thanks," I told Ted Bradshaw.

"I got honey, too."

"Ditto."

"Artificial sweetener? Got Sucaryl, got Sugar Twin, got saccharin."

"I'm fine," I said. "Thanks."

It was by far the longest conversation—perhaps it was the only conversation—we'd had over years of being colleagues and neighbors.

And then I found myself alone in my office, scanning the *Home* magazine puffery idealizing and romanticizing me and my loved ones. I knew these people well; I was one among them. Yet I read the article as if it were some anthropological treatise regarding a lost tribe from Java or Jersey or Jupiter.

In another moment my door opened again. I looked up expecting to see Bradshaw but instead found myself staring at Ginger Kenton. "You're not finished yet?" she asked me starkly.

"Good morning to you, too," I said, setting down the paper on the floor at my feet, draining the last of the best coffee I had ever tasted in my life, and placing the cup on my windowsill. Slowly and deliberately, I swiveled back to my desk and allowed my fingers to hover above the typewriter keyboard.

Furiously, I commenced typing. "FADE OUT," I said aloud as I typed. And then I typed and said, "The End."

I ripped the page from the machine, slapped it atop a script-sized stack of pages beside me.

"Is it any good?" Ginger asked me, worried.

"You tell me," I said, shoving the typescript at her.

She picked it up and skimmed lightly through it, now and again actually smiling, here and there even chuckling. "Looks good," she said at last, nodding.

"Congratulations," I said to her. "I'm proud of you." The horror is that I actually meant it.

"Why, thanks," Ginger Kenton told me brightly, shrugging with gosh-all-golly modesty.

Casually, ever so matter-of-factly, she reached high in the air with her arms and wriggled out of the two-dollar thrift-shop halter she wore, standing before me bare-chested, her girlish breasts bobbing scant inches from my face. "What are you doing?" I asked her.

"What do you think I'm doing?" she asked me back.

She stepped from her sandals, undid the top two of four brass buttons securing the waist, and slid her jeans down to her ankles. Involuntarily I stared directly at her neat, rude tuft, at once downy and satiny soft yet also bristly-woolly. One leg at a time, pointing her toes, she stepped from the denim folds gathered at each ankle.

I gulped and stammered and, at last, reached clumsily for my phone. "What are you doing?" she asked me curiously, squinting, as I twisted the dial on the antique rotary instrument provided senior faculty. "Campus Security," I said into the mouthpiece.

"What do you think you're doing?" she said urgently.

I told the telephone, "We need an officer right away at—" but Ginger stepped toward me, plucked the receiver from my hand, and replaced it in its cradle.

Without a word, she began putting on her clothes. "When you change your mind," she said, buttoning her pants, "let me know. You've certainly earned the consideration."

" 'Consideration,' " I said. "Is that what you call it?

"Love," she said. "Sex. Humping. Call it what you will."

"I call it preposterous. Pitiful. Pathetic." And after a moment I could not resist adding, "And those are just the p's."

"What's preposterous, pitiful, and pathetic is this little charade we're enacting right now." She dragged the halter over her head and down across her torso. Her face emerged at the other side of the stretchy cloth tube and she said quietly, "We've toiled closely together on a creative enterprise. It's inevitable we're to be lovers."

"You've got everything all figured out."

"The issue stands between us," she said, "whether we recognize it or not. We can ignore it or we can confront it, but in either case it looms there like a third person in the room." She was dressed now, except for the sandals. She allowed them to remain where they were on the floor. "You're a man," she said. "I'm a woman. We ought to get the whole bloody business over with, just to have it out of the way. Until we do, it stands between us like the Berlin Wall." She paused for a moment, then added, just a little wistfully, "You're not the least bit attracted to me?"

"I'm a married man," I said.

"A married man is not a dead man."

"I would never hurt my wife's feelings."

"Why would she have to know? If you love her, you'll see to it that she doesn't." She shook her head slowly. "Does she respect your own feelings when she balls lovers of every gender and hue on every movie she's made?"

"You read too many tabloids."

"She didn't fuck and suck her way through film school? She didn't bang the chairman? She didn't flap her cheeks on screen and hump that African dude? You've never seen *Extra Hot Sauce*?"

"Someday you'll understand the difference between reality and illusion."

"It's merely an illusion she's gobbling Slade Sloan's dick? She's only pretending to sit on his pole, to spread her butt cheeks and ride him up and down, until it's running slick and slippery with steaming streams of semen?"

"And selling seashells at the seashore?" I asked her.

"Excuse me?" she responded blankly, altogether missing my extraordinarily clever allusion. I instantly forgave her. She had her youth, which is to say she lacked the maturity to appreciate so professorial an insight. "You're positively obsessed with sex," I told her quietly.

"I say there are two people in this room right now positively obsessed with sex."

"Ginger," I said, going into my adult responsible-educator mode, "I like you. More than that, I'm extraordinarily fond of you. You're a devoted, disciplined talent with a shrewd sense of showbiz savvy. You're full of fun and energy. You are thoroughly, beguilingly delicious."

I hesitated, pausing in order to allow the substance, the import of my message to sink into her consciousness. Stunned as I was by her behavior, I was also actually touched by her attentions, however clumsy and awkward. I calculated that it would be a mistake to reprimand her harshly, that my duty was to let her down gently without suppressing her artistic spirit. "I'm your teacher," I told her. "It means that there is a truly special nature to our relationship, even if it precludes certain activities, even if it places upon both of us some cruel but realistic and necessary limits. Can you understand that? I know that you can."

She looked down at the floor with what might have been embarrassment, perhaps even contrition. She seemed for a moment truly to be the young girl she surely was.

"As an educator," I continued ever so patiently, "I have to judge you objectively, I have to maintain a certain distance, if I'm to render dispassionate evaluations of your work and faithfully to fulfill my charge and to discharge my duties as teacher and artist."

She sighed and nodded and actually seemed to understand. She looked up at me and smiled weakly. She stepped back into the sandals, one at a time, and turned to leave.

She reached for the doorknob.

"Wait," I cautioned her as she was about to depart. "One last thing," I said. She turned and looked me in the eye and waited. "See that moosehead coatrack over there." She looked at the rack.

"I want to see your clothes hanging from it right now."

She shrugged and began once again to strip off her clothes, draping the garments one at a time upon the antlers.

Recklessly, I pulled off my own clothes and with a single broad motion of my arm swept to the floor the piled books and papers and paraphernalia obscuring my frayed off-white-and-wheat-weave Indian cotton couch.

We collapsed together in a fleshy tangle on the sofa. We crushed each other to our chests, knotted together our various limbs, crawled and swam around one another naked on the couch.

Soon enough she settled astride me; first my face, then my groin.

She was something of a gasper, if not quite a screamer, and I was myself, in fact, uncharacteristically noisy, grunting, groaning, panting, moaning. All the while various items crashed from nearby bookcases and assorted shelves.

In the midst of it all, I noticed Professor Ted Bradshaw's coffee cup still gracing my windowsill. I thought of the old codger sitting there in his office, slugging down his coffee and eggs and reading the Sunday paper, and I realized that with all the sweet and heady racket he might as well have been sitting right here in the room with us.

Such behavior on my own part was, of course, quite simply shameful, impolitic in the extreme, uncollegial, unprofessional, disrespectful, and a host of other things.

And about all that I cared not a whit.

43

"**the envelope, Please?**" **DEAN** Greene pronounced with the obligatory dramatic flourish.

A hundred elegantly dressed (except for one) souls drew a collective breath, and I actually felt my ears click in response to the drop in cabin pressure. I half expected oxygen masks to tumble from the ceiling. We sat at the edge of our ranked, padded folding chairs in the plush Easton West Center at the campus's south end.

The Mayer Foundation's silk-bloused and blowzy director of public affairs took her sweet time—here was the moment each year for which the sherry-swizzling old biddy lived—handing over the sealed document. At last the dean plucked it from her hand. He paused yet another moment, smiled broadly, and scanned the room.

I scanned the room myself and spotted, among others, no small number of my colleagues, including Professor Ted Bradshaw in his familiar pajamas and bathrobe, the outfit he had now taken to wearing both night and day. Present also was nitro-popping now emeritus Gordon Michaels. My wife, the celebrated film artist Veronica Baldwin, had never looked more radiant. There was also a host of students, the finalists, many among them now snacking voraciously upon their fingernails.

And there were university officials in plenitude: deans, associate deans, chairs, chairmen, chairwomen, chairpersons, vice chancellors and associate vice chancellors up the wazoo. And there were scattered movie bigwigs, especially agents.

Present, finally, were members of the press. Their cameras rolled as the dean said, "This year's scriptwriting competition winner is . . ." Privately I lamented that he called it scriptwriting; there was something trivializing in the characterization. Silently I ruminated over the issue while the dean lingered still further over what should have been the simple enough challenge of opening an envelope. At long last, having milked the bit beyond all toleration, he ripped the seal and removed the envelope's contents in a single smart and snappy motion.

". . . Ginger Kenton!" the dean proclaimed with glee, as if his fondest wish had come true, as if he had been, as I was myself, eagerly rooting for this particular candidate even if she was, at least to him, a total stranger.

Ginger, wearing not a skimpy miniskirt but an actual dress that dropped clear to her actual knees, gasped and looked down at the floor, then up at the ceiling. She turned to hug a man approximately my own age, a plain-looking polyester dude seated beside her. And at last she arose and navigated her way through the narrow aisle, accepting with kiss-kiss aplomb the insincere good wishes of her classmates and competitors.

She arrived at the podium and basked in the applause. Gradually the cheers died and silence descended upon the chamber. Not fumbling a bit with the microphone, in a soft, clear voice she spoke. And what she said caused me to experience substantial excitement.

"Before I say anything else," she told the assembly, "I must assert that there is a man here without whose support, encouragement, inspiration—and simple good faith—I could never have written 'Alley Rats.' " She paused for a breathy breath. I trembled in surprise and gratitude.

"He is in so many ways a self-effacing man, a modest, gentle soul, who himself detests attention and credit for what is properly, duly his own, yet I hope we can all of us together here today on this most special occasion coax him into taking a well-deserved and sorely overdue bow."

My heart swelled with pride. Damned if my eyes did not grow just a trifle moist. I made a clear and hasty judgment that it would be impolitic for me to weep, even for joy. As my leg muscles tightened in preparation to stand, as my torso bent forward and my hands gripped the chair's edges readying to propel me skyward, Ginger Kenton said, "Will you rise, please, Daddy?"

Simultaneously, I and my contemporary, the man who occupied the chair beside Ginger's, both rose to our feet.

And after a confused, excruciatingly awkward moment, I replaced my butt in my chair.

I made a clear and hasty judgment that it would be impolitic for me to vomit, although I was overcome with nausea.

Ginger Kenton's genial, nice-enough father nodded sheepishly to the group, and all except me applauded with polite enthusiasm. It occurred to me, several frames later, as the applause was finally dying, that I, too, ought to applaud and so I started to clap my hands. And as all others quit clapping I clapped ever more vigorously until I was all alone clapping like a madman until Veronica reached over and gently covered my hands with her own, stifling my now-solo performance.

"Bullshit!" a voice called out as the room returned otherwise to silence and Mr. Kenton to his seat, and I was enormously relieved to realize after a moment that the voice was not my own. "Bullshit, bullshit, bullshit!!!"

Fire in his eyes, spittle foaming around his lips, crazed and crazy Warren Robbins, the student who had created the near scandal weeks earlier in my office, stood tottering at the edge of the room. A dreadful hush fell upon the chamber.

Robbins, thoroughly beyond any semblance of control, stumbled several steps forward. "That trampy little tit-twirling twat doesn't deserve any goddamned award!" he bellowed like a yak, his voice lowing, squeaking, cracking, sputtering with rage. "She's been balling the judges! It's a fucking fix, don't you know?"

He let it all sink in and, after a moment, continued. "I see her day after day, everybody sees her, hanging around with this guy," he said, gesturing vaguely toward me, "who just happens to be one of the judges, tailing him like a puppy dog. Either they're lunching intimately in Westwood Village or she's sitting patiently in his office, her nipples stiffening, his chops drooling, her pussy moistening, her labia glistening with her own special brand of rank, rancid cunt juice."

The speaker paused for breath. In the roaring silence that followed, the dean muttered privately to an aide, who swiftly departed the room.

"First prize?" Warren Robbins's maniacal laugh reverberated like a loop from a horror movie track or an antique haunted-house ride at a decrepit other-era amusement park. "First prize for what? For humping? For sucking cock? You kidding me? Look at her! Look at her! You can see the imprint of his schlong on her lips!"

The previously meek, sheepish Mr. Kenton, Ginger's recently honored dad, again departed his chair, this time far more swiftly. He rushed to where Robbins stood, and lunged at him. In another moment the room was awash in flying chairs, smashing wineglasses, and soaring canapé trays as the crowd attempted to separate the two.

I distracted myself by pretending it was all a scene out of *Brutal Bad-ass Angels*.

44

THE SAME FLUNKY WHO'D earlier scurried off to summon the gendarmes to haul Robbins away now poured rare old sherry from a lead crystal decanter into fluted vessels, from which all in the room over the age of twenty-one—that was everybody besides Ginger Kenton—sipped. Ginger guzzled Perrier, which was at that time still really rather a new phenomenon.

Ginger and her dad, I and Veronica, and Dean Greene sat on couches and in overstuffed chairs in his surprisingly—for a public university—plush and spacious oak-paneled office. The dean was finishing what he clearly hoped would be his final statement treating the distinctly unpleasant subject.

"And finally," he said, "I wish personally to take responsibility, and to extend to all parties my humblest apologies." He looked at Ginger and her father, and he looked at me. "The university in general, and I in particular, regret that our security procedures were insufficient to such an extent that the young man in question"—the dean slapped his reading glasses onto his face and peered at a document—"Robbins," he said, and then removed the glasses, "happened to crash the ceremony. The fellow possesses, incidentally, a long and sorry record of disruption and mental illness. He suffers from stress, apparently, due to his family situation." The dean put on the glasses and squinted again at the document. "Says here his mother's got colitis."

"But that's absurd, Dean," a voice said, and this time it was very much my own. "Respectfully," I hastily added.

"Professor Thomas is quite correct, Dean Greene," Ginger said quickly in an attempt to head me off. The young woman knew me well enough already—in some ways better than I knew myself—to anticipate, and also to deplore, what I was about to assert.

"Although we understand and welcome your generous spirit, Dean Greene," I continued undeterred, "I must also insist that none of what has transpired is in any way the university's fault."

"Professor Thomas is quite correct, Dean," Ginger's dad said.

"Nonsense," the dean insisted. "Robbins should never have been allowed on campus. Not after that shabby incident in your office, Stu, when Security had to be called."

"That's best forgotten," I agreed, "but . . ."

"And this, too," Ginger's father insisted, "should be forgotten. I'm proud of my little girl, and while it's unfortunate the ceremony had to be marred, it doesn't really change a thing."

There was a brief, sharp rapping and before the flunky could respond, the door to the dean's office swung open. There stood Professor Ted Bradshaw, clad in his ratty bathrobe. "Pardon me for interrupting, Dean Greene," Bradshaw said, "but I ought to let you know that I occupy the office next door to Stuart, and I want to offer some information for your consideration."

Ginger and I both stiffened with apprehension as Bradshaw moved now fully into the office. The flunky shut the door behind him.

"I'm there pretty much all the time in my office," Bradshaw said. "The walls are paper thin, and I hear everything that goes on next door." He repeated for emphasis, "Everything." He waited a moment as Ginger and I traded a covert, anxious glance.

"Like," Bradshaw continued, "if Stu farts, I hear it. I can practically hear the guy think. I can hear his fucking fingernails grow, if you'll pardon my French. I assure you that if something had gone on, I'd know it. If he were harassing students, I'd know it. The plain truth is that he's never once acted inappropriately in any manner."

"We know it, too, Ted," the dean said. "But we're grateful for your support."

Bradshaw turned to leave.

"Hang on a second, Ted," I insisted. "You don't have to lie for me." I turned to Ginger. "Your life," I said to her gently, and then I faced Veronica, "and yours, too, can be a catalog of falsehoods if you choose, but my own," I asserted with overflowing dread and pomposity, "can tolerate not one more lie."

Veronica's eyes narrowed in dismay. "You mean you really hit on that guy, what's his name, Robbins? You made a pass at him in your office? You're gay?"

"Of course not," I said. I wondered whether Veronica was intentionally missing the whole point. And I also wondered why in the world, given our long years together, I had chosen this particular moment to confront her.

"This really isn't anybody's business," Veronica said to me almost in a whisper, scanning the faces in the room, embarrassed. "It's about time, Stuart, that you realized the connection between art and love. You engaged in a dalliance with a fresh young artist. What's so dreadful about that? You want me to be jealous, and perhaps in some corner of my consciousness I am. But most of all I commend you for connecting in a visceral way with new talent. Perhaps now you can be a little more understanding about some of my own such connections from time to time and years ago."

"Connections?" I asked Veronica. "Is that what you call it?" She was so damned understanding. What would I have given for her to cry out in anguish at my disloyalty, to weep an angry tear or two, to scratch out my eyes? Instead, she sat there proud, beaming, apparently pleased with all she had learned.

"This meeting is adjourned," the dean said, rising.

Turning to the dean, I confessed, "I did not hit on that boy. But I did make love to Ginger Kenton in my faculty office." I turned now to Ginger's father. "I'm sorry," I told him. "I'm truly, truly sorry."

Mr. Kenton looked at me, mildly surprised. "You owe me no apology," he said. "Ginger's a big girl. Today's kids, who can figure them? Their lives—including their sex lives—are their own." He hesitated a moment and then he added, "Perhaps it's your wife here to whom you owe an explanation."

"Not a bit," Veronica said calmly, without a trace of anger or bitterness. "Stuart and I have been together fourteen years. What we have is too solid to be threatened by any mindless fling with a coed." She turned from the others and looked directly at me and only me. "I would forgive you, darling, if I thought you'd done something wrong."

"But I did do something wrong. Many things. Besides betraying our marital trust, I entered into an unholy relationship with a contestant whom I was bound to judge objectively, dispassionately." I paused mightily before proceeding. "It's a clear case of sexual harassment, to say nothing of a conflict of interest."

"Nonsense, Stu," Dean Greene said quickly, trying to calm the situation. He seemed annoyed, not by what it was I claimed to have done but, apparently, solely by the claiming. "The guidelines for harassment and conflict of interest are plain enough. It's got to be more than a casual sex act. It has to be unwelcome. Most pertinently, there's got to be an express and explicit quid pro quo. Tit for tat, so to speak." The dean hesitated for another moment and then added, apologetically, "Maybe that's an unfortunate way of stating it."

Looking at me, he continued, "Would you have viewed her script differently if the sexual relationship hadn't occurred?"

"Definitely not," I insisted. "It's a first-rate screenplay."

In a tentative voice, Ginger said, "Dean?"

The dean settled back reluctantly into his chair. Ginger turned to face Veronica. "Ms. Baldwin, it was I who seduced your husband, not the other way around. It was wrong of me. He vigorously resisted. Forgive me for the offense I have surely caused you. You're the model of all I ever hope to be. I want as a film artist merely the tiniest fragment of what you have yourself achieved."

Veronica reassured Ginger. "That's sweet of you, really it is, but don't give it another thought. It's okay."

I turned to Ginger in disbelief. "First Bradshaw lies for me," I told her, "and now you?"

The dean again rose to his feet. "Meeting adjourned!" he announced now as if to a full faculty conference.

"I ordered her to strip naked," I told the dean, my colleague and campus neighbor Professor Ted Bradshaw, my wife, my student-lover, my student-lover's father. "I instructed her to hang her clothes on my moosehead coatrack."

"But I had already volunteered to do so," Ginger said. "I had already stripped off my own clothes and stood before you stark naked in your office. I flashed scant inches in front of your face. You tried to stop me. You attempted to call Campus Security. You insisted I get dressed."

"I insisted you get naked."

"Dressed," Ginger said.

"Naked," I said.

"Dressed."

"Naked."

"I'm not going to allow some petty squabble over a quick, purported, alleged roll in the hay," the dean interrupted, "to besmirch the reputation of the Mayer Foundation, which just happens to endow this college for a pretty penny. This motherfucking meeting," Dean Greene insisted uncharacteristically, "is motherfucking adjourned!"

45

i WAS A TWiSTeD, discombobulated, confused, and nervous
wreck, not only in spirit and soul but in flesh and bone; my neck
ached, my back was in perpetual spasm. Pains shot up and down
my butt and into my legs. I could barely stand. I could barely sit. I
could barely lie down. I could sleep not at all.

In desperation, I turned to the needle.

Traipsing through the darkest, scurviest corner of L.A.'s old Chi-
natown along Ord Street—not the gussied-up shiny plastic tourist
trap on North Broadway below Dodger Stadium—I peered at the
address scrawled on the scrap of paper that my contact had provided.
I sought an address on the doors of decrepit tenements of another
era, but there were no numbers to be found.

At last I spotted in a dusty storefront window the hand-scrawled
sign: "King Kwong, Ping Pwong, and Associates—AcuPuncture R
Us, a Service of AmFac, A Wholly Owned Subsidary of Special
General Enterprises, Second Floor." I jangled the knob; it came off
in my hand, and the door swung slowly open. I hobbled up the
steep, dark stairs and arrived finally at Master Li's etched, frosted-
glass door; both Kwong and Pwong were on vacation, Li explained,
and he was covering for them.

In testimony to the amount of showbiz clientele this office served, there was a stack of recent trades: *The Hollywood Reporter* and *Variety*. While Li spent several minutes on the phone talking to his bookie, I scanned the tattered papers and noticed no fewer than five references to my daughters. They'd each fallen into one aspect or another of the movie business, Pacifica then interning for Don Simpson's company at Paramount and Raynebeaux working as a reader for the new agency Mike Ovitz had formed after splitting from the Morris Office.

It was called Creative Artists Agency. I thought about the names of agencies. I vowed that if I ever opened a talent agency, I would call it Pretty Good Artists or Moderately Promising Talent Group.

Soon enough I lay naked on the table as Li burnt herbs and heated his array of long, slender needles. My whole life I had suffered from a needle phobia; that I now actively sought relief via needles marked the level of my desperation.

At last, Li wielded and manipulated his weapons. I had been told to expect instant relief; instead, I cried out in pain.

"Relax, will you?" Li said with a native California hey-good-buddy! air. "The needles never lie. There's something bugging the living shit out of you. Am I right? Well? Am I?"

"Help!" was my only response as he jabbed me rudely somewhere beneath the lung.

"There!" Li exclaimed brightly. "I felt it right there! There's something going on. A bad relationship, that it? A marriage? A girlfriend?"

I lay in silence. I had not schlepped this distance—well east of Doheny—in order to make small talk.

"Your silence," Li said, "is the most eloquent articulation of the righteousness of my proposition. So, confess it. Is it a wife or a girlfriend?"

"Ouch!" I said as Li manipulated his probe. "Okay," I said, seeking mercy. "Yes."

"Yes?" Li said. "Which? A wife or a girlfriend."

"Yes," I said again, "a wife or a girlfriend." When I saw that the answer did not satisfy Master Li, I added, "I'm not sure which."

"Aha!" Li said. He left a needle dangling below my armpit and inserted another between a couple of ribs. "You must choose!" he said.

"Okay," I agreed, attempting to placate my tormentor. "I choose."

I said this purely as a tactic devised to escape the premises; I would have sprung from the table and fled, stark naked, down the steps, taking them four at a time—except for the fact, of course, that I could move hardly at all. At this point I could not even bend down to tie my shoes and had given up, therefore, on the costly Adidas I'd worn since the time they were still called sneakers. I had taken to wearing loafers because you didn't have to tie them.

If I had the physical ability to flee, why would I remain another minute with this quack? Was it not pain, after all, that had brought me here in the first place?

"Say it like you mean it!" Li insisted.

"Okay!" I shouted at him as well as I could, what with my face squished sideways against the stainless-steel table. Summoning all the enthusiasm I could, I said again with my heart and groin, "I choose!"

And now, no sooner than I had said it, I found myself totally, thoroughly, miraculously healed. The pain dissolved like sugar in hot tea. It wasn't only that the pain was simply gone; in fact, in all my days I had never known such serenity.

"You're right!" I rejoiced. "I've made my choice. You've compelled me to make my choice and I've made it and now I'm free!

Free of pain! Free to live my life as it was truly meant to be lived! I feel quite perfectly tranquil! Good God, what you're doing right now, it feels just great! You're a fucking genius, Li."

AccuPuncture Master Li abruptly ceased his ministrations and just as abruptly the agony—physical and spiritual—returned.

"Hey!" I said. "Why'd you stop? Don't stop! Please don't stop!"

"Sorry," Li said, "but that's all the time we have for today."

46

"MACKEREL? SQUID? EEL? OCTOPUS?"

"Yuck!" Ginger Kenton grimaced like a teenager and tossed her reddish-brown-rinsed mane. "None of that crap for me, thanks just the same." She flopped her broad, bulky bag onto the table in the cozy, narrow booth, rattling the silverware and teacups, spilling some sake. She fidgeted with the zipper, managed at last to slide it open. From the bag she withdrew a Big Mac and a large order of fries. She jammed a fistful of the latter into her mouth and, before chewing or swallowing, bit off a substantial portion of the burger. "I came prepared," she said through the mouthful of food.

"You should have told me you don't like sushi."

"Why? You obviously like it or you wouldn't have asked me here."

"I hate the stuff. I was trying to impress you. Sushi's big now, don't you know? How do you expect to make it in the movie business if you don't eat sushi?"

The waiter arrived at the table with a large combination of assorted selections of costly raw fish and raw fish eggs. The pumpkin-orange salmon roe shone bright as neon. I calculated that each minuscule egg cost about a buck forty in George Bush dollars. He set the platter down between us.

Of course Ginger did not touch the sushi, but then again, neither did I. Instead, I reached into my pocket, withdrew a small, velvet-lined jewel box, set it on the table, and shoved it straight across to the young woman.

"For me?" Ginger asked.

"For us," I said.

"Us?" She looked at me curiously, then down at the box.

"Open it," I encouraged her.

She hesitated a moment and then, the Big Mac in one hand, she manipulated the wrapping with the other, somehow tearing off the ribbon, lifting the cover, and exposing the contents. From the box she removed now a bright, shiny key. She regarded it mysteriously.

"Want to take a ride over there right now?" I asked her.

"Over where?"

"Our place."

"I don't get it," she said, chewing the burger just a bit more slowly.

"I'm moving out of my house. I've taken an apartment."

"And you really feel it's appropriate for me to have a key?"

"A key to your own apartment?"

"My apartment?" Ginger looked at me in total confusion. Shaking her head, she said again, "I don't get it."

"Idiot!" I laughed my too-good-natured all-wise all-tolerant tenured-professorial laugh. "We're moving in together!"

"But that's impossible," Ginger said.

"Why? Because I'm a married man? There's a difference between a married man and a dead one." I smiled at her and thought that surely I was entitled to have at least a little smile in return. Instead, Ginger sat there looking increasingly confused, and also grim. "Besides," I added, "I'm getting unmarried. I see a lawyer tomorrow."

Ginger shook her head slowly. At last she said, "Veronica never said a word."

"Since when are you speaking with Veronica?"

"Since she acquired the rights to *Alley Rats*."

"What in the world are you talking about?" I asked her. Panic and dread rose in my heart and clutched at my throat.

"She read the script and wants to do it. It's her next picture." Ginger resumed eating, taking another hefty bite of beef. "The deal memo's already signed. There's just a bit of boilerplate that needs to be ironed out. There's a slight hang-up over definition of net profit, but the business affairs guys seem to be coming around. There's a bit of last-minute wrangling over sequels, spin-offs, ancillary considerations, that sort of thing, but it's likely to be all cleaned up soon enough."

I was numb. Had I hallucinated the whole exchange? Veronica had said absolutely nothing to me of Ginger when I revealed to her that I was planning to leave. I would have suspected that this was some sort of sixties acid flashback, except that in all the brilliant stupidity of that era I'd never once dropped acid. I tried several times to speak but could think of nothing whatsoever to say. I made a couple of gurgling, choking false starts that amounted to not much more than the grunts and groans and clicks and hisses of a stroke victim.

For lack of anything else to do, I mindlessly watched my hand, as if it belonged to another individual, a stranger. On its own, the hand reached for the large platter of sushi. Arbitrarily it plucked a generous, moist morsel of maguro—unsalted, undercooked, overpriced tuna resting on a bed of sticky rice—and tossed it whole into my mouth. Without any enthusiasm at all, my mouth made motions that vaguely resembled chewing.

"Stuart," Ginger Kenton said between bites of her Mac, "I like you. More than that, I'm extraordinarily fond of you. But you're my teacher. I don't want to spend my whole life in film school."

"You mean like I'm doing," my voice mumbled through the rice and fish.

"There's no way I can thank you properly for all the attention and consideration you've shown me," Ginger said. "But I can't support you in this horrific course: abandoning your family, trashing your life, all in the name of some unresolved adolescent fantasy."

If what she said made perfect sense—and it surely did—it struck me, also, as perfectly cruel. Tears welled up beneath my lower lids, partly in sorrow and perhaps also in anger. But I decided it would be impolitic for me openly to weep, so I suppressed the urge and, instead of bawling like a baby, not yet having finished the food that was still in my mouth, I popped yet another portion of sushi inside, where it joined the first.

I made several more chewing motions, and then halfheartedly attempted to swallow. The rice and the sweet, stringy fish went partway down one dry pipe and then lodged firmly in the other.

I could not see myself, of course, but I could see Ginger, and I saw her react to what must have been the change of color in my face; I expect I turned linen-white and then, perhaps, purple-blue and, ultimately, slate-gray. I know she was impressed, because for the first time she actually set down the hamburger. "You okay?" she asked me. "Stuart? Stuart?"

At the same time as I attempted to smile and reassure her, I keeled over in the chair and collapsed in a heap on the floor. "Stuart!" Ginger shrieked, and it was the last sound I heard.

And the last sight I saw was Ginger Kenton, rushing toward me, thank God, straddling me, pressing hard against me with her hands in a sincere if misdirected effort to save my life.

47

AFTER GINGER'S OWN INJURY—the blow to her head—had been detected and the paramedics had abandoned ministering to me in favor of herself, I likely lay ten or fifteen minutes more on the floor of the Hama Yoshi Restaurant before the second team arrived. By this juncture Ginger had long since been removed to the hospital.

The new team worked over my lifeless form for a decent interval—the precise period their protocol requires—before declaring me deceased and summoning the coroner. Soon enough I was eased into a body bag and zipped up as snug as a bug in a rug.

They wheeled me out into the pale drizzle and around to the rear of the Black Maria. They opened the double doors and slid me onto a metal shelf. Had I been alive I might have noticed another couple of occupied bags on another couple of such shelves.

If the ambulance bearing Ginger had sprinted recklessly, siren screaming, with me the coroner took his time and why not?

Certainly there was nothing resembling any hurry.

Moreover, given the mist, the streets were uniquely hazardous as they inevitably become in Los Angeles when it rains not heavily but lightly. A thorough downpour flushes the cumulative oil drips of a trillion cars and leaves the pavement pristine and relatively steady. A mere smattering of moisture, however, settling into the asphalt's pores, coaxes the oil to the surface. This renders the streets slick as ice, and it's one of the two reasons that the tiniest workaday sprinkle wreaks full-fledged havoc in Southern California.

The other reason, if the truth be told, is that behind the wheel Californians are wimps. How else to explain the need for traffic signs reading DO NOT STOP ON GREEN?

And so my driver, in eloquent testimony to his responsibility and circumspection, took his time, negotiating the streets with extra care, even if for my own particular sake it mattered not a whit.

Nevertheless, at Virgil and Sixth, opposite Carl's Jr., a lost, wretched woman started suddenly from the heap of papers, cans, bottles, and rags that happened at the moment to constitute her residence. In response to demons unseen, without warning she fled across the street, directly in the path of the coroner's wagon.

The driver jammed on the brakes and the wheels promptly locked. The vehicle swerved this way, that, tipped over to one side, and then as if orchestrated by a movie stunt coordinator, it righted itself, tilted to the other side, then finally spun a perfect three-sixty, skidding a solid half block until smashing into a light standard and coming to a clanking, smoking, leaking halt, half on the curb and half off.

The bodies in the rear all flew from our shelves and landed in a tangle on the floor.

Miraculously, the shock of the crash, the collapse of my shelf, and the collision with other bodies in the wagon had the effect of partly dislodging the spoiling, rancid plug in my esophagus. Now, perhaps solely through lingering neuro-electrical reflex, my flesh heaved and twitched. And now, somehow undead, I coughed. In the blackness of the bag I puked and jerked, gasped, sputtered, swallowed.

I breathed.

Awakening to total blackness, I took some dreadful moments to realize it was not blindness but solely the effect of being zipped into an opaque body bag. I scratched frantically at the fabric and was able really rather easily to poke a pinky through the loose end of the zipper, seize the tab, and zip myself free.

The rear door of the wagon hung by a single hinge, and I had no trouble pushing past it and out into the street.

Before anybody but the few gathered homeless folks could arrive to gawk, I was on my feet and could very well have been taken for just another schizophrenic bystander. As God is my witness, one of them hit me up for spare change.

I obliged, handing him whatever my fingers found in my pocket, perhaps eighty cents.

I waited for a bus to pass. On its side panel was an advertisement hawking Veronica's latest movie. Raynebeaux had worked on it as a production assistant. It was a sequel to an adaptation of a comic strip that had been scripted by one of my former students and was becoming a most lucrative franchise.

Casually, I strolled off into the night.

I walked for some several hours through the damp, dark night. And I would say that I wandered without direction, but that simply cannot be the case as it can surely be no accident that eventually I found myself at the deserted late-night/early-morning UCLA campus and, in particular, at the Department of Film and Television.

I made my way past the softly glowing bank of vending machines lining the walk at the back entrance to Macgowan Hall and climbed the dark exterior fire stairway to the third floor. I approached my own door quietly, anxious to avoid disturbing Professor Ted Bradshaw's beauty rest.

I pulled out the staples securing my Instructor's Door Card just outside my office, fondled the document for a moment, then crumpled it and let it fall to the floor. I scratched around in my pocket and found the key, and for the last time I let myself into my office. I scanned the premises in the dim light from a distant street lamp to see if there was anything I wanted to salvage.

I hefted my moosehead coatrack over my shoulder and made my way back out into the corridor, out onto the exterior landing, down the fire stairs, and into the night, which was just now slowly dissolving to day.

48

i **left not only** film school but also my marriage. "Hollywood loves a role," John Milius had told me decades earlier when we were still classmates at USC. "They want you to play your role." John was himself underneath it all merely a kid who calculated that in the flower-child peace-and-love let-it-all-hang-out sixties there was room for a purveyor of hair-on-your-balls blood-and-guts war-is-fun fare.

He believed in none of it, of course, but managed a substantial career pretending. He pretended among other things to be a hard-boiled surfer, when even merely driving down the Pacific Coast Highway made him seasick.

But what are movies, I asked myself silently, if not pretense? Are movies not the ultimate pretense in all of human history? What jockeys and juggles time and space, shakes and shuffles shadow and light, arranges and rearranges character and story in the manner of a movie? In movies, actors pretend to be people they are not; they pretend to speak dialogue as if they just now thought it up when in fact, of course, it is scripted, memorized, recited. Throughout the known and unknown universe, what could possibly rival motion pictures for pretense?

I realized that my own role in the Hollywood community had evolved over the years to become inextricably, irrevocably enmeshed with that of the professor. I had become an *éminence* prematurely *grise*. I wasn't the guy to write the movies. I was the guy to nurture the guys writing the movies. *Variety* actually anointed me the Jewish Mother of Screenwriting. I could kibitz and consult, cuddle, coddle, reprimand, scold. I could cook chicken soup and I could rap knuckles. Sometimes I did it for free, out of the goodness of my heart.

Often, however, I did it for substantial fees. I had become known throughout Hollywood as Mr. Notes. In a dark and crazy way, I had been awarded the power to green-light pictures. I had the distinct feeling that I could make virtually any picture a reality, except, of course, one written by me.

Fees, schmeeze, a writer is not what I was; a writer was what I was not. I was too old to be a young talent. Now I was the alter cocker who nurtured the fresh talent. How in the world could I have expected to be taken seriously as a writer if I no longer took myself seriously?

Exactly as a writer firing his agent hopes for at least a ghost of resistance, a murmur of protest, I was devastated when my bride of more than two decades was all too intelligent about the proposed separation. I would not have minded a bit of pleading, a bit of begging for reconsideration and reconciliation. I would not have minded the slightest expression of reluctance.

Instead, upon my broaching the subject, Veronica barely turned her head from the TV, where amateur videotape footage played out depicting four Los Angeles police officers beating a motorist nearly to death. The damned clip played over and over and yet Veronica's fascination with it seemed only to increase.

With respect to the proposed dissolution of the marriage, she was so reasonable, so totally understanding, so agreeable, expansive, and accepting that I was sick to my stomach and retreated to the bathroom to puke blood. God forgive me, but for the briefest moment, coolly and seriously I considered torching our manse.

Why should Veronica have felt or acted otherwise? I was taking absolutely nothing. I planned to buy all new stuff. I wanted to start life anew. I recalled years earlier how my erstwhile boss, Jerry Lewis, wore brand-new underwear fresh from the wrapper every single day. His drawers were never laundered; they were merely discarded.

Once I had privately mocked him for it; now it was an inspiration.

I left the west side and became my own former tenant's tenant downtown. The real estate syndicate that had purchased my artists' lofts years earlier now rented me a cramped studio. It was a fairly expensive place, even when calculated in Bill Clinton dollars.

It was the place where I wrote and also lived, sleeping in a cot in the corner, bathing in the motel-style sink. At night, when the poets and painters and sculptors were gone, I had the toilet down the hall to myself.

All the while, reports of Hollywood's impending demise proved woefully wrong. The movie business was in fact exploding.

The major studios, I came to realize, were really but a fringe. Where for years they had been the beginning and end of everything, they were now merely the beginning. What Sid Sheinberg had created at Universal during my brief tenure as a writer under contract, the Movie of the Week, now outnumbered studio production by a factor of four or five.

I churned out scripts for them. The basic theme was always the same: Women in Jeopardy.

Moreover, the VCR had transmogrified the nation's viewing habits, and I was able to produce scripts for the direct-to-video market. These movies were also distributed theatrically abroad. There was an insatiable craving all around the world for American films. Any old story, plus an appearance by a washed-up TV actor—say, Erik Estrada or Ernest Borgnine—was a done deal in the European, Asian, African, and Latin American markets.

And the newfangled cable systems, designed at first simply to improve reception in outlying areas, were quickly becoming whole studios all by themselves, producing their own product including oodles of original feature films and scads of opportunities for free-lance screen scribes such as myself.

I admit it: Like all the other writers in Hollywood, regardless of whatever they tell you, I still hoped for that breakthrough, mega-budget, big-studio excess but was happy enough plinking and plunking along on my new word processor.

I'd been writing now for a solid quarter-century. My decrepit, CPM-based, coal-fired, spring-wound twin-floppy Kaypro II (64K onboard RAM) had given way to a Gateway 2000 machine that possessed its own hard drive all by itself containing three whole megabytes of memory. And that was now replaced by a setup with capabilities such as zip drives and MMX technology that I didn't even pretend to understand.

I was really rather startled one morning when there was a tentative rapping at my studio door. I was in the midst of finishing a romantic comedy financed by a consortium of Germans, French, and Italians, and was on a hard deadline. The movie it was to be called *Woman in Jeopardy* and told the story of a woman in jeopardy.

"Who is it?" I barked.

In fact, it was a movie producer from a major studio who was eager to see me and had made an appointment a week earlier. I had completely forgotten our date. Her voice was fuzzy through the riotproof heavy metal door. "Who?" I complained again.

The door slowly swung open and I faced my own darling daughter, Raynebeaux, now a splendid ebony figure fully glorious in her young womanhood.

49

"**YOU SAID YOU'D CALL** first," I told my daughter.

I had stayed in touch with the girls over all of these years, of course, enjoying irregular but steady contact. Still, it astonished me to see Raynebeaux all grown up, a poised, charming, responsible young woman who also happened to be as beautiful as a movie star. I recalled how her mother and I would carry her in a wicker basket into Barragan's, our favorite Mexican restaurant, during our Echo Park days. Could it have been more than twenty minutes ago?

Yet here she was, a woman on her own, threading her way through hulks of burnt-out cars, driving over broken glass, passing homes and stores still smoldering from the insurrection that had followed the four LAPD officers' acquittal in their Simi Valley trial. She virtually took her life in her hands, all for the purpose of spending even just a little while with me. "Respectfully, Dad," she said, "a daughter shouldn't have to make an appointment for a visit with her own father."

"You said this was business. Even with family, business is still business. I'm on a deadline here," I complained, looking at her over my shoulder from the vantage of my glowing phosphorescent screen.

"Deadline on what? Some cockamamy cable feature starring Louise Lasser or Sharon Gless for a month's run on systems in Louisiana and Guam, to be followed by theatrical distribution to Guyana and Nepal?"

"Also Morocco, Uruguay, and Luxembourg," I said, "with additional markets lining up every day, the producer tells me. But, Raynebeaux, you are now yourself a producer, are you not?"

"At Paramount. Dawn Steel's in charge. A woman, can you believe it? Running a studio. She's opened the floodgates to fresh, fertile, female talent. She hired me for two reasons. The second is that I'm full of ideas and creative energy."

"The first?"

"Mom attached me as a condition of her own deal. I've got an office, a phone, and an assistant, plus a substantial discretionary development fund."

"I'm proud of you, doll," I told my daughter, totally sincere.

"Why?" Raynebeaux challenged me. "You're always saying the studios are a hellhole of cowardice and conformity."

"Aren't they?"

"They used to be. Were they ever any worse than some rinky dink cable outfit putting out pictures on budgets that wouldn't cover breakfast for the Teamsters on a real movie?"

"It's not a real movie if it doesn't cost a hundred million dollars? Raynebeaux, darling, listen up. These cable movies, these direct-to-videos, they're the new B pictures. They're the arena where true film artists can reach and stretch, experiment and grow and be creative."

"The forty-fifth woman-in-jeopardy picture is reaching and stretching and creative?"

"I'm not talking about major TV network Movies of the Week, with scores of vice presidents and development executives looking over your shoulder, running focus groups. I'm talking video and cable. If you bring it in on time and budget, and if it's in focus, and if somebody bothers to set the f-stop, you're pretty much free to do whatever you want. Artists can dare to try stuff out. They can risk making mistakes and falling on their faces because an entire multinational conglomerate isn't riding on this one picture."

"Do you think someone like Dawn Steel came to a major studio simply to replicate what the old boys' network has been doing year after year? She's sick to tears of sequels and prequels and remakes and adaptations of supposedly safe projects derived from other media like novels and magazines and comic strips. Trust me, Dad. Here's a woman who understands that the most reckless thing you can do in movies is play it safe." Raynebeaux peered past me at my computer. And at precisely that moment the screen saver clicked in, depicting a pattern of swirling, spiraling ellipses. I was privately pleased she had not seen what was on the screen, since it was a sequel to a remake of an adaptation of a minor novel that had enjoyed modest success around the globe several years earlier as a comic strip.

"I can tell you this much," Raynebeaux said at last. "Whatever Dawn Steel has in mind, I can promise you Raynebeaux Baldwin-Thomas did not sign on at Paramount just to do what everybody else does. I want to produce original projects that resonate with humanity, that express the hearts and souls of the artists who create them." She hesitated. "And for my first project, Daddy, I want to hire you."

"Me?"

"Yes."

"And precisely what original, creative project do you want me to write?"

"The studio's hot to do a major-budget movie; they'll spend seventy or eighty million."

"On what?"

"They want to remake *Brutal Bad-ass Angels*."

50

the Remake of Brutal *Bad-ass Angels* eventually was produced, but only after bouncing around from studio to studio to studio. After a flurry of false starts and dropped, picked up, dropped, picked up, dropped options, a bidding war broke out among studios that five minutes earlier had not even existed: Cinergi, Fine Line, Miramax, Carolco, Fox 2000, and DreamWorks SKG. Thanks to some clever poker-playing by my representatives, the fees were preposterously generous.

I hated what ultimately happened to my script. Under pressure from actors and producers and directors and agents and actuaries and accountants, the *Brutal Bad-ass Angels* sequel story line writhed and twisted like a serpent and was bent all out of shape. The thematic truths with which I'd imbued it were warped way off their marks. Ultimately I tried to take my name off it, but ended up getting screen credit all the same.

To my dismay, the picture won critical approval, but did a quarter of a billion worldwide all the same. Of course, this caused *Brutal Bad-ass Angels II,* also *III, IV,* and *V.* By that point the studio started to worry about fitting so many Roman numerals on a marquee, particularly at a multiplex, and so the next several editions were called *Return of Brutal Bad-ass Angels, Revenge of Brutal Bad-ass Angels,* and so on. This was followed by a retreat to the Roman numerals: *Return of Brutal Bad-ass Angels II* and *III* plus, of course, *Revenge of Brutal Bad-ass Angels II, III,* and *IV.*

And just for fun, or perhaps because of a printing error in the videocassette cover art, they skipped *V* and went straight to *VI.*

My hardest job was not writing the movies but pretending to take them seriously. This became increasingly difficult as the franchise acquired a following that consisted of billions of people all around the world. Worst of all, film scholars, theoreticians, and historians were accrediting the installments with praise that was quite simply pathological: "Bends back the borders of the medium." "Redefines the language of the cinema." "Asserts and articulates a bold new paradigm for filmic form and function." I nearly fractured my face trying to hold my cheeks together as commendation after commendation rained down upon me like incoming mortar straight out of the Tet offensive just about a generation earlier.

Most amazing of all, I was now making more money than Veronica.

On this particular day, with poor Dawn Steel now several months in her grave, the new millennium practically upon us, I sat hunched before my new machine, a Morrow Micro-Design Decision Data Digitizer 9000QX. It had a Pentium IV chip that ran at 600 megahertz; it finished writing some screenplays even before I'd quite thought them up. The damned thing had so many bells and whistles that it could not only handle multimedia, interactive, and digital but also roast, grind, and brew coffee and, so help me, vacuum the tattered carpet in the little loft I continued to rent from my former tenant.

While the size of my computer's memory had increased exponentially, so, also, had that of my prostate. A new question had been added to my annual checkup: How's your stream? A man truly comes of age when it takes him longer to pee than to do the other thing. By guzzling gallons of cranberry extract and popping saw palmetto pills and selenium tablets like M&Ms, I managed to keep my nocturnal bathroom visits down to as few as one or two an hour.

I sat there that afternoon in my homey hovel, traffic crawling around the eastbound Santa Monica–northbound Harbor cloverleaf, sketching out notions for—God forgive me—a memoir, its working title *Misadventures in the Screen Trade or How to Die of Encouragement in Hollywood*. I leaned back precariously in my swivel chair for just a moment and hitched up the too generous waist on my rented After Six tux.

In the background the radio played the mantra of the O. J. Simpson trial. I had it tuned low but could make out the voice of Johnnie Cochran saying, "If the glove don't fit, you must acquit."

A positively stupendous sentence that I was about to key into the computer—writers no longer wrote, we now merely keyed or entered or input—evaporated like steam, thanks to a polite but insistent rapping at my door. "Who is it?" I called. The door opened and the chauffeur, whose immaculate uniform cost more than my tux, leaned in and informed me that the block-long limo was ready.

Who needed a limo? I could have roller-bladed, I could have walked from my office to the Shrine auditorium near my old haunt, USC. I was met at the same time by Pacifica, who this evening would accept the prize for *Return of the Revenge of Brutal Bad-ass Angels XII* as Best Picture. We were seated next to Ginger Kenton, who would offer a wonderfully articulate speech upon her copping Best Director honors for the film. I admit she'd made my pathetic script shine.

When they opened the envelope for Best Screenplay and announced my own name, I made my dazed way to the podium. There was actually a standing ovation. When the crowd settled down I realized it was my own turn to say something.

"First of all," I said, "I want to thank the members of the Academy. Surely there can be no greater honor than to be celebrated by one's own peers." I said that because that's what everybody says when they win an Oscar. Then I spoke just a little more. "This is just great," I said, "really great. But I really, truly have to pee."

Although I had told no joke, affectionate, roaring laughter shook the room along with a 2.8 aftershock of the Landers quake. Through an ocean of applause I made my way to the auditorium's magnificent Moorish pale-green-tiled men's room. I positioned myself before the sculpted, gleaming porcelain urinal, which beckoned me like a blossoming vulva.

I took my life's greatest leak.

51

DURiNG ONE OF the frequent and interminable recesses in the proceedings, I slipped past the reporters and photographers gathered outside the courtroom and made my way to a cramped lawyers' conference room down one floor and off the main corridor. There I whipped out my Maxxitechnix HJ-4009 laptop—it had more memory than all my previous computers combined, its four full ounces fitting neatly into the palm of my hand—and worked on the latest *Brutal Bad-ass Angels* installment. Legal niceties aside, the studio was paying me a fortune to keep going, as if monumental copyright questions were not pending.

Eventually the proceedings resumed and I found myself back in court at the defendants' table. In the witness box sat the plaintiff, Warren Robbins, the student who'd tried years earlier to frame me for harassment.

His attorney, Pierce O'Donnell, placed both hands on the railing as if for theatrical effect. But anyone could see that the three-hundred-pound lawyer was sincerely trying to support his weight.

The jury's attention, it seemed to me, focused upon nothing but that rail. How could they not have been preoccupied, as I was myself, worrying that the polished-walnut banister would at any moment splinter, crack, and transform itself instantaneously into sawdust?

"You trusted Professor Stuart?" Pierce asked the witness.

"Absolutely," Warren Robbins asserted.

Here the litigator took one of his signature dramatic pauses. Pierce O'Donnell was reigning master of the dramatic pause. I don't doubt he'd majored in the Dramatic Pause when he studied law at Penn perhaps forty years earlier. He posed, postured, primped, preened for judges and jury and mainly, the gallery. And at long last he returned his attention to the witness.

"And you were confident, when you handed in your class assignment—your screenplay—that it would be safe in his hands?"

"Completely confident. I never imagined he would snatch my idea, run with it, exploit my toil and creativity for his own self-aggrandizement, retitling the script *Brutal Bad-ass Angels*, slapping his own name on it, robbing me of both my credit and the remuneration properly due me." Robbins seemed to recite rather than speak the lines, as if they had been scripted, rehearsed, memorized.

"That is so preposterous as to defy comprehension," I said when my own turn came several days later. "I can't believe this is happening. I wrote *Brutal Bad-ass Angels* years before I met the plaintiff. Years before I began teaching at UCLA. How could I have stolen something that didn't even exist?"

"Yet you opine repeatedly in your screenwriting classes that what is special about film is the way it addresses . . ." Here Pierce paused, his voice trailing off as he lowered his reading glasses from their perch atop the pompadour fronting his gray wave. He picked up a copy of a book that I could see from my vantage on the stand to be *Meaning in the Visual Arts* by Erwin Panofsky. Pierce peered closely at a page and now read aloud, ". . . the spatialization of time and the dynamization of space."

"I do?" I asked. "I opine that? How can that be? I don't even know what it means."

"Don't you agree that film jockeys and shuffles and arranges and rearranges and choreographs and orchestrates time and space as no other form of expression does?"

"I beg your pardon?" I could not figure out what in the world Pierce was talking about.

"In film, time is relative, is it not?" Pierce O'Donnell asked me. "There are flashbacks and flash-forwards and jump cuts and the order of events is never really clear. Aren't films shot out of sequence? Isn't everything basically interchangeable?"

I had no earthly idea what Pierce meant. "I have no earthly idea what you mean," I told both him and the court.

"Professor Thomas," Pierce said, looking up at me with something like melancholy. Here I was, gone from the university for several years already, but I was forever the professor. I did not particularly mind being addressed by that title in light of the vast power film professors had acquired over a generation in Hollywood.

"Don't you ever feel even just the tiniest taste of remorse," Pierce wheezed, phlegm rattling in his lungs like coins in a blind man's cup, "for violating your sacred covenant as an educator, for stealing your student's idea and turning it into a billion-dollar movie-and-merchandising franchise?"

Before I could respond, five defense attorneys were on their feet vociferously objecting. One represented the studio; another had been retained by the agency; one represented the packager; still another represented the production company within the studio that had made the movie; and one even represented me.

The judge, doing his Lance Ito impression, called for the forty-fourth sidebar. Soon witnesses, defendants, and spectators were cooling our collective heels.

An hour later the announcement was made: A settlement had been agreed upon by all parties, its terms to remain confidential.

But the terms were promptly leaked to me and made me burn white-hot with rage. Robbins was awarded a cool million dollars, plus something far more valuable than that: one half of one percent of the ancillary considerations belonging to the entire *Brutal Badass Angels* franchise: toys, comic books, tunes, beer mugs, theme park rides, plus technologies not yet invented and to be named at a later date. It made him the 679th-richest person in California, according to a *Fortune* study.

"Why in the world did you give him anything at all?" I asked the studio's representatives.

"He was your student and you had access to his material."

"That doesn't mean I stole it. That hardly establishes infringement."

"We have here on one hand a rich Hollywood studio and on the other a lonely, oppressed, impoverished writer. We can't take a chance that a jury will feel sorry for him and award him a mercy judgment, possibly a far more substantial chunk of future revenues. Besides," the lawyer added, "it's all covered in our errors-and-omissions policy."

"And what in the world does that mean?"

"It means," the lawyer patiently explained, "we're insured."

52

"ONE FINAL QUESTION," FILM professor Ginger Kenton instructed her class. "Our guest has been extraordinarily generous with his time. Just one last question."

Nevertheless, not one but three questions popped out of students' mouths in virtual unison:

"How do you get an agent?"

"Do you word process or work on ruled yellow pad in longhand?"

"Do you negotiate ancillary considerations—novelizations, spin-offs, coffee mugs, toys, and accessories—simultaneous to copyright?"

The questions, frankly, appalled me. "These questions," I said, "frankly, appall me."

I stared back at the faces that stared back at me now in silence. "Isn't anybody interested in the spiritual, emotional, intellectual aspects of writing? Are there no questions on character, story, dialogue, scene structure, language?"

I nodded curtly, turned on my heel, and left the classroom. Ginger, more alluring than ever in her mid-thirties, called out "Class dismissed" behind me and quickly followed my route down the Sloan Hall corridor. It was one of the new buildings, named for

Slade, now ten full years in his grave, merely one more victim of AIDS.

She caught up with me and walked by my side through the sculpture garden. We traveled some distance in silence, and then, after a good long while she pronounced the word: "Yes."

"Excuse me?" I asked her.

"Yes," she said again.

"Yes?"

"Yes. I'll marry you."

"You're playing some sort of game with me."

"I'm dead serious. I know it's a bit of a jump cut, but years ago you asked me to marry you." She looked down demurely at the exquisitely landscaped knolls and the carpet of spent jacaranda petals. Then she looked up at me with those long lashes that fluttered so assertively, so seductively, as to stir the slender branches of the weeping willow that had leaned protectively over a steel Calder mobile for perhaps four decades.

"I'm ready now," she said. "At long, long last, I am ready."

I reminded Ginger that I had never quite gotten so far as formally to propose marriage to her. I explained that she might well be ready for marriage but that I, myself, was not.

On the way to the parking structure we passed East Melnitz, where all the windows were dark except for that of Dean Veronica Baldwin. Even with the blinds drawn, the shadow of her figure was plainly visible, hunched at the desk over a computer at the same time as she pressed a phone to her ear and yak-yakked in what could only be her airy, earthy, convincing way. Even without hearing the words she spoke, I could tell she was talking somebody into something.

I extricated myself from Ginger and headed for Parking Structure Three where Big Irish, the lad who'd accompanied me on my original VW Beetle ride to California, awaited in the limo. I told him to take his beer belly back to the studio: I'd catch up with him later. There was someone I wanted to see.

I marveled to contemplate that I now had sufficient clout in Hollywood so that if I changed the Three to a III, I could pitch the damned parking structure as a sequel and win a rich development deal.

As for Irish, the lath-and-plaster hustle that had brought him to California decades earlier had collapsed with the introduction of drywall to the building trade. He ended up buying real estate during the boom years, creating land syndicates, earning quite literally hundreds of millions of dollars before cashing out just before the late-eighties realty crash. He speculated recklessly in strategic metals—titanium futures indexes—and made yet another bundle. He ended up buying the old Goldwyn lot and creating his own multinational media conglomerate.

He was now my boss.

I took a detour around the School of Social Welfare, sneaked behind LaValle Commons, and found the precise manhole cover. I nudged it out of the way, climbed down the ladder into the air-cooler tunnel, and made my way to Professor Emeritus Ted Bradshaw's cave. They'd forcibly retired Ted—he was the last to go prior to the abolition of compulsory retirement—and booted him from his office. He'd retreated first to a storage closet in the Macgowan basement and ultimately to the maze of utilities tunnels beneath the campus. He thrived there as if nothing at all had changed.

"Yo! Stu!" he greeted me. "Cup of tea?"

"I'd be grateful," I told him.

"Orange pekoe? Chamomile? Peppermint?"

"Surprise me," I said.

Ted poured boiling water from the pot on the hot plate into the cup, over a fresh bag of something or other. I settled into a weary, comfy rocker beside my old moosehead coatrack, which I'd awarded Bradshaw a couple of years earlier when I'd commenced making these occasional visits. I passed the while with my esteemed friend and beloved colleague, sipping tea and swapping war stories.